Andersen Prunty

Grindhouse Press

CREEP HOUSE

Horror Stories

Also by Andersen Prunty

Sociopaths In Love

The Warm Glow of Happy Homes

Bury the Children in the Yard: Horror Stories

Satanic Summer

Fill the Grand Canyon and Live Forever

Pray You Die Alone: Horror Stories

Sunruined: Horror Stories

The Driver's Guide to Hitting Pedestrians

Hi I'm a Social Disease: Horror Stories

Fuckness

The Sorrow King

Slag Attack

My Fake War

Morning is Dead

The Beard

Zerostrata

Jack and Mr. Grin

The Overwhelming Urge

To Carrie,

You are the best pet ever.

and

To the Kids,

Thanks for being who you are.

CREEP

HOUSE

Contents

THE CALMING WOOD

A man named Figg wandered across several states searching for a certain geography. That was the only way he could really think of it. He was not a spiritual man. He'd led a rough life. Always, he found himself in a town or even just a piece of wilderness or countryside, and eventually he had to move on. But his back had begun twisting up on him and he trembled even when he tried to stand still. The grinding sound in his head had become unbearably loud. If he found his special place, he didn't think he'd be moving on.

There were some thick woods in these parts but, already, farmers had begun clearing away the trees to make room for fields to plant crops. Farming was becoming a big business.

Living off the land by killing it. That was no way to earn a living. The man didn't think *working* was any way to make a living. He'd made do without a job most of his adult life. His memories of childhood were cloudy things. His father had made him work despite Figg being a sickly child. If there was ever a day Figg wasn't able to, his father had him make up for it the next day.

One morning Figg stumbled onto a narrow dirt road. It was relatively flat and he could see farther then he'd been able to see for days. It looked like it was going to be a perfect spring day. It was about time. Here it was the middle of May almost and he'd bet it hadn't reached seventy until a couple days ago. The sky was a sweet, brilliant blue, puffy white clouds hanging still like the exhalations from a kind god that didn't exist in Figg's world.

And under that perfect sky, the landscape rose slightly and the already narrow dirt road seemed to disappear in shadow. The man knew that was the place. Somewhere cool and dark and quiet, like a grave above ground. The man didn't like the sun and the light the way he used to. Hell, even then he'd only seen it as something like a cleanser for his late nights. The things he'd seen and done in the shadows were best left there and while he managed to thrive in that environment, there'd always been a part of him that looked forward to waking up in a sun-filled room. He guessed most people were supposed to like the light and warmth more as they got older. Common belief held that a warmer climate would make his back feel better but it just made him feel like more of an ailing, monstrous old man. It was like lighting a lamp in a filthy room, the grinding in his head there to match the frantic scurry of cockroaches.

He moved so slowly it took him all day to reach that shadowy place on the horizon. He traveled south on the road, the sun stinging his right side. But even that began to diminish as he moved closer to the woods. At first he thought maybe it was already sunset and the sun had tucked itself beneath the earth for the night, but there it was hanging in the sky. It should have been intense but, somehow, it wasn't. It was like, not even in the woods yet, the shade was already keeping the sun from him. This was a good sign.

A small furl of smoke climbed out of the woods and dissipated in the sky.

Now he even had an exact destination.

He reached into his pocket and pulled out his knife and sharpening stone.

Someone living all alone in the woods like that . . . Well,

Figg thought that person was probably a lot like him. Meaning he probably wouldn't be missed and maybe even had a reason to be living so far from people.

Figg just hoped it wasn't a family. It wasn't that he would feel any guilt. Figg had heard that word – guilt – but had never experienced the feeling. When there were more than one or two people, he tended to like it too much. He really lost himself in it and usually paid for it the next day. It had been a while since he'd had to do it but the memory of last time was still quick to bubble up.

When he finally stepped into the woods, it was like all the crazy nattering in his head went silent. He'd once taken an apartment next to a glass blower's shop. Every morning, Figg would be woken up by the sound of the man sweeping glass shards out of his shop. Until then he'd never really had a close comparison to the sound that was almost always in his head. It lessened a little around nightfall on any given day and quieted almost completely if he was staying in one of his good places. The only time it stopped was when he did what he felt like he was born to do. And, well, probably when he was sleeping but he was unconscious and couldn't enjoy the silence then. A tree falling in a forest with no one around and all that.

He paused to take it in. If it wasn't so welcome, he may have thought of it as eerie. He didn't hear any birds or insects or animals, although he could see them.

He was locked into his path, gliding through the dim woods, sharpening his knife on the stone and not hearing the gritty sound of the blade becoming more lethal.

He spotted the dim glow from the cabin just as the light seemed to die completely from the air around him. There was a yellowish window, probably lit by a candle or a lantern. There wasn't much of a clearing. Like whoever had built this shoddy, ramshackle cabin had cleaned out only enough trees to fit it. Figg liked that idea. He never could understand the concept of a yard. Wide open spaces only made you more vulnerable.

There was a single crooked step before the door.

Figg knocked on the door and waited. He heard footsteps and slid the sharpening stone into his pocket, tightening his grip around the haft of the knife.

The man who opened the door was black and this momentarily surprised Figg, but not enough to derail him.

The man looked just as surprised to see *him* but Figg was sure to make eye contact and say what needed to be said:

"I've come to take up residence here."

He heard his own voice from a distance and it didn't feel like it came from him.

The man looked slightly confused but before he could even back away, Figg had already slashed the knife across his throat. Figg had done this enough to be sure he'd done it correctly but it was hard to see the blood against the man's skin so he didn't feel completely confident until he saw the front of the man's grayish shirt turn dark. Once he saw that, all the sounds of the natural world came back to him. The brain sound stayed away.

Figg could have continued stabbing but didn't know exactly how long he was going to be here and didn't want to damage more of the body than was necessary. The man dropped to the floor and clutched his throat. As long as he didn't have a gun on him or within arm's reach, Figg didn't figure he had much to worry about. Mostly he just stood where he was and tried not to get too much blood on him.

Figg surveyed the tiny shack in the dim glow. He was wrong about the candle or lantern. The fire was the only source of light in the room. Maybe the man had been asleep already. He wondered why he'd just opened the door like that. It seemed like he should have been a little more cautious. Maybe he'd been expecting someone. That didn't make

Figg as nervous as it probably should have. Maybe this man just wasn't running from or hiding from something like most of the black men Figg had encountered. The fireplace looked like a good one. There was already a metal rack for cooking in it. Most of them didn't have that. A relatively comfortable, though narrow, bed was pushed into a corner. The man probably lived alone. There was a wobbly table against the wall below the solitary window. Figg was grateful to look up and see a sturdy beam running through the center of the room. Various pots, pans, and burlap sacks hung from it. Figg poked a couple of the sacks until he came to one that, hopefully, contained what he wanted. He lifted it from the nail and glanced into the opening. Salt. A lot of it. Good. He suspended the sack back on the nail. He didn't want it to get soaked with blood.

Figg unspooled the rope wrapped six times around his waist. He must have lost some weight on this latest journey. His pants almost slipped off his hips. He waited for the man to stop flopping.

When he was pretty sure the man was finished, Figg bound his ankles with one end of the rope and took the other end over the beam. He hoisted the man so he hung upside down. A steady trickle of blood continued to pour from his throat. Figg secured the rope around the beam and made a slash along each of the man's wrists. He'd wait till the man had bled out before splashing the floor with a pail of water. The house wasn't constructed particularly well and he was pleased to see most of the blood already finding its way to the earth from in between the floorboards. It wasn't overly hot so he didn't think he'd have much to worry about. He was tired. That bed was starting to look pretty inviting. He'd earned a good night's rest. Tomorrow he'd get up and begin the carving. Hopefully he'd have everything ready to start drying and curing the meat for the day after that. He wasn't sure how much it would yield. It would probably be more than enough. And if he ever got sick of eating it, he could probably find a town to sell some in and maybe make enough for some steak and eggs. He usually told folks it was ostrich jerky so they didn't have anything to compare it to.

Figg fell asleep to the soft thick drip of the man's blood.

When he woke up early the next morning, the man was gone.

That had never happened before.

Figg inspected the rope coiled on the floor. It didn't look ripped or shredded at either end. Supposing the man could have lived through the bloodletting – a feat Figg was pretty sure was not possible – maybe he could have chewed or gouged the rope loose. But given the shape of the rope, that definitely was not the case. Something like that would had to have woken him up, anyway.

The front door was open. Figg walked outside and looked around. If the man had managed to free himself in some fit of post-death strength, he couldn't have gotten far.

The trees greatly diminished visibility, but Figg didn't see the man lying on the ground or any sign of movement.

Given the unsecured nature of the rope, the open door, and the fact there wasn't a trace of the man, Figg could only think of one solution: someone had taken the man – a member of his family or something. Hell, maybe even someone like Figg. Someone happy to discover most of the work was done.

Just thinking about his loss made Figg's stomach rumble.

He went back into the tiny shack and found two potatoes on the brink of going bad in a wooden bin near the fireplace. He cut them up, fried them in a pan, and ate them outside while sitting on that crooked step and surveying the dark shadows of the wood. The potatoes didn't satisfy his growing hunger but they'd have to do for now.

In the distance he heard a dog bark and a little girl scream.

He guessed if worse came to worst, he knew where to go.

Last night he'd had his plans for today all worked out but now he found himself with nothing to do. He decided to explore the woods even though he knew his body would make him pay for it the next day. He never worried about getting lost. His sense of direction was perfect. Once he'd locked the location of this shack into his head, he could walk a thousand miles away from it and still know where to return to should he decide to turn around. There were a number of tall dark pine trees mixed in amongst the elm and oak and maples, which was odd for this part of the country. Not that Figg minded. He liked the gloom they produced. A damp chill hung in the air and he imagined there was a river or creek somewhere in the area. A ready source of fresh water was always a good thing. The shadows and the perfumed air put him in something of a spell as he spent the majority of the day wandering through the woods. He didn't stumble upon any more houses and when he thought about returning to the shack it took him longer to find it than he thought it would. He cautiously approached it. What if the man or a member of his family had returned to find it empty? What if they had decided to take it back? Figg had his knife ready as he slowly opened the door. He surveyed the small space and found it empty and exactly as he had left it. When he took a jug of water out to the step and sat down, he saw the black man wandering through the woods. He had the carcass of a dog slung over his shoulders and clutched the hair of a bloody and mangled girl's corpse, dragging her through the dirt and dead leaves. Figg again removed his knife from his pocket and clutched it hard in his hand, feeling the closest thing he'd felt to fear since his father had beat it out of him.

The man didn't seem to notice him. Figg watched him shamble through the woods with no attempt at stealth, burdened by his dead cargo. Figg knew there was no way this man could be alive. What Figg had done to him last night was something he'd done countless times before. Many times he didn't even bother making the incisions on the wrists. He'd only done that because of the man's size and possible virility. So how was it this man had managed to free himself? How was it he now managed to walk amongst the living with enough vigor to take the lives of others? Figg had heard about certain black magic practices and rituals. He'd lived throughout the Deep South and in some of the poor areas of this country's larger cities where those sorts of beliefs were common. But even good old Christianity had its belief in a number of strange, dark fantasies. Figg had avoided all of it. Now the mere thought of it sent tendrils of unease uncoiling through his body. This man, this creature, was shattering the calm wood he'd found. Already, Figg could hear the grinding glass sound. It was faint right now, but he knew how it would go. It would start at the top of his spine and slowly infect his whole head until he moved on to some place else.

Unless he kept on top of things.

Unless he could trap the man and destroy him.

He wished he'd paid more attention to what those believers had said.

Figg went back into the shack to search for a gun. Someone living all alone out here in the woods was almost certain to have one. But if this guy had kept one, Figg couldn't find it. Maybe he hadn't needed one. Aside from hunting and killing, Figg reasoned the gun's existence was due to the fear of death. A man kept a gun, ultimately, because he was afraid of dying. So, he reckoned, a man who couldn't die would have no need of a gun.

But how did he hunt?

The imagined answer to that question made Figg nervous.

He could see that man, that thing, wrapping his large hands around the dog's throat, taking a deep and savage bite from its jugular, snapping the girl's neck when she came to the aid of her pooch.

Some men sure were sick, ferocious bastards.

Figg had trapped both men and animals before. Okay, so usually he'd trapped women and those he kept around for more non-dietary purposes, but he felt confident he could do the same with this . . . creature. The only way to get rid of the thing once and for all would be to completely destroy the body. First he would sever the head and burn that. Then he would sever the rest of the limbs and feed them into a roaring fire. He would find the creek running through the woods and dispose of any remaining bones. And if the grinding glass sound didn't go away, he would move on. He might have to move on anyway, if he couldn't manage to find a lasting source of food. He would have to remember to start decapitating his supply. And also maybe destroying the head just to be on the safe side. He didn't really enjoy the brains and eyes much anyway and the neck muscles were always tough and stringy.

The man had now shambled out of sight.

Figg supposed he could have gone after him but his walk had left him feeling tired and listless.

The day was practically done anyway. He withdrew inside. He nailed a board across the door, removed the legs from the table, and nailed that over the single window. He didn't really know if he'd be able to fall asleep or not but, if he did, he didn't want to wake up to that thing's teeth at his throat. Figg found a small pipe and a pouch of tobacco in a tin on the mantle. A quick inspection of the leaves revealed that it wasn't tobacco but maybe an herb or a weed. Figg decided to smoke it anyway, thinking it might diminish the grinding sound. The only things he knew to stay away from were the mushrooms some of the Indians liked and the consumption of alcohol. Both of those made his thoughts too weird. They made him lose the tight self-control that had kept him alive all these years. The mushrooms had made him think he was a god and the alcohol just made him tell everything to whoever would listen. He was lucky that the one time that had happened, the person he had told all his secrets to was trussed up and in the process of bleeding out. No lasting harm there.

After smoking, he lay in bed and stared at the shadows on the ceiling. He'd neglected to start a fire and was happy it wasn't very cold. He went over his plan again and again. Maybe he should just get out. What was stopping him from doing that? Nothing, really. That would certainly be the easiest thing to do. He could try to get a decent night's rest and head out that door first thing in the morning and hope like hell he didn't run across that thing creeping through the woods. But he knew he wasn't going to do that. This man's resurrection had been something of a defeat to Figg. He didn't like to lose. It was one of the reasons he'd never joined the ranks of decent society. He wasn't on their playing field and would have lost repeatedly because he didn't have the proper skill set. He wouldn't have even been able to take the small daily failures. He would have probably ended up in jail. Just to prove he'd beaten his father once and for all, Figg had carried the man's severed penis in his pocket until he'd lost it during a month-long bout of youthful indiscretion.

He woke up the next morning unaware he'd even fallen asleep. He drank some water and pissed into the fireplace. The pain in his back was excruciating and the clamor in his head was back with a vengeance. The door and window seemed to be unmolested. He pried the board off the door. The dead man had left something for him.

In front of the step was the carcass of the dog with the little girl's head in place of its own. The hair was dirty with leaves entwined in it and her milked over eyes stared right at Figg. Beyond this creation was another one. A stake impaled the girl's body between the legs. The dog's head sat atop her body. Both creations were crawling with flies that Figg couldn't hear over the deafening roar in his head. He went back into the shack and shut the door.

The things outside bothered him in a profound way. In a number of ways, really. Figg had, over the years, made it a habit to kill people so he could eat them. It seemed like a rational, pragmatic, although perhaps ghoulish, thing to do. There had been some women he had had to kill to keep them from talking. He had usually ended up eating them, too. He would never describe anything he did as senseless or mindless. Not that the constructions outside were completely mindless. He thought there was definite intent there. Which brought him to another thing that worried him. Killing a black man who lived alone in the woods was one thing. Now he had the corpse of a little girl and her dog outside the place he'd overtaken. Not just their corpses, but their mutilated and molested corpses. Even Figg thought it was sick and he had a pretty bizarre code of ethics. Whatever was happening with the man he'd killed was not normal. Maybe he should invent a clause allowing him to leave without feeling as though he'd lost some battle. As far as he knew, he'd never had to deal with the supernatural before.

But he knew he wasn't going to leave.

He still had some rope.

He could build some kind of trap with that. Snag the monster around the ankles and dismantle him before moving on. Maybe he could even salvage the meat from the girl and the dog and plant himself here for a while. After all, he'd need sustenance and if he planned on staying, he'd need to get rid of the evidence. People *would* come looking for them. He guessed he'd go out and get started on the trap right away. If he stayed cooped up in this shack all day waiting for that thing to come back, he'd go insane.

He smoked some more of the herbs and took the rope out into the woods.

He'd need a sturdy branch.

This time, passing the jumbled corpses and walking into the woods was like submerging himself in the ocean. Maybe the clamor was still there but it was pushed down to a level just above audible. He heard nothing else and seemed to be only aware of his surroundings by about a three-foot radius. He reached up and tested some branches, searching for the right amount of spring and sturdiness. He'd been here less than twenty-four hours and nothing that had happened had seemed right. He'd seen many strange things but nothing as strange as this. The rope trailed in the dirt and brown pine needles. He thought he saw the monster man at one point and froze up. Figg couldn't go after him. What would he do if he caught him? There was something off about this place. He knew he'd sought it out, wandered until he found somewhere that felt good to him. Someplace that felt *right.* This had always worked for him. He'd always had success. Like a farmer finding the right plot of land he'd always had a good yield and managed to pull out before he got caught. He'd never attributed anything otherworldly to this ability, just experience and instinct. It was like a transient's education. But he was starting to think there was something about this place that had seduced him, even lied to him. He knew he should get out. He should definitely get out. He shouldn't even bother returning to the shack. There wasn't anything of his in there anyway. Nothing he really needed. He should keep going. Follow the sun west. Go all the way to the ocean. Maybe even sign on with some kind of vessel and go someplace far away like China. No place would be far enough away from here. Maybe not even the heavens. But even as he thought this, he was wrapping the rope around a branch and testing its sturdiness, creating a sort of slipknot with the other end.

He saw a man walking toward him. It wasn't the monster. This was a white man. He held a rifle. His mouth was moving but Figg couldn't hear anything coming out. He dropped the rope and reached for his knife but something had him around the tops of his arms and he didn't even realize it was another man until yet a third man reached into his pockets and emptied them of their contents and when he did this Figg's pants almost came down and he was pretty sure his cheeks colored with shame and, like that, all the pain and all the sounds came back and it was like exploding to the surface of the green ocean.

"Stay still!" the man in front of him shouted.

Figg noticed the badge.

The man behind him bound his wrists behind his back.

"What is all this? I didn't do nothin!"

Figg refused to walk so they dragged him over to the dirt trail that would eventually lead into town.

The road was lined with unspeakable atrocities.

The monster had been very busy.

It was tough for Figg to hear the men over the noise in his head.

The school had gone on a field trip to the woods.

No one had returned.

Worried parents.

What kind of sick man does this?

Blood and limbs and flies everywhere, lining the trail like a road of horrors.

The trial was short. Many of the parents cried for hanging. The sheriff agreed with them. Mr. Elias Figg should certainly be hanged. He should probably be drawn and quartered. Possibly even castrated. But the judge had a better idea. Twin Springs was new. It was going to be a growing village, maybe even a town or a city one day. There was work that needed doing. There certainly wasn't a lack of volunteers to oversee Mr. Figg in his labors. And if ever he should escape there was certainly no lack of volunteers to go looking for him and bring him back.

There was always someone there to watch him. Even when he was alone in his cell, there was someone watching him to make sure he did not take his own life.

Figg lived a lot longer than he ever imagined he would.

He managed to escape a number of times but never got very far. The repercussions were always very severe.

Now a very old man, every part of his body screaming with pain, he managed to escape and make it all the way back to the shack in the woods. No one had reclaimed it. It was a haunted place and, while it had been somewhat battered and abused over the years, it had never been lived in or destroyed. Still free, Figg struggled up into the shack – the step had long since rotted away. He lay down in the middle of the floor and stared at the shadows moving across the ceiling. He didn't think about everything he'd done and not done. He closed his eyes and did the one thing he'd come here to do in the first place.

MAY TO MAY

Zena Rado knocked on the door and waited. She slid the key into the lock and opened the door. This was always the part she found most thrilling. The rest of it was exciting in a different way. The excitement of discovery. Like the kind an archaeologist on a dig might have. The initial discovery – unearthing – of the way these people lived was a shot of pure adrenaline.

Sometimes there wasn't anything at all. Sometimes the house was simply empty. As it really should be. Nothing except an old scrap of paper or toothpick shoved into the back corner of a kitchen drawer. But this was rare. Most people left something behind.

A few of the tenants had been hoarders. This, other than the obsessiveness of their condition, offered little clue as to any specific personality. It was just the compulsive acquisition, almost randomly, of stuff. The only thing their hoarding really said about them was that they were consumers, and possibly more sentimental than most. Or they were just lazy. Most people in our modern world were consumers. The only real difference between a hoarder and the rest was how one curates and displays her acquisitions.

More often than not, she found the perfect balance of things taken and things left behind. This helped her form a far more accurate life of the tenant who'd lived at 523 Glowers Pike, Twin Springs, Ohio 45---.

Alan Beaumont was an example of this type of person.

Zena had to check the lease in her hand to make sure she had his name right. Even though she'd opened his checks for the past twelve months, the name had eluded her.

She stepped into the dining room through the door in the carport and breathed in the familiar musty earthy smell. One of the tenants had complained about a mold problem a few years back and they'd had to take care of that. Like everything her parents did with their rental properties, it was done cheaply and half-assed. Sometimes a tenant would manage to successfully tamp down that smell that made Zena think of a grave but it inevitably came back. It wasn't an odor she would describe as a stench. She found it pleasing, comforting, woodsy.

Everything was in her parents' name. Zena handled things while they wintered in the Florida Keys. Their winters were getting longer and longer. And why not? They were getting older and, having lived most of her life here in Twin Springs, Zena had heard many people refer to the "damp chill" that seemed to hang around nine months out of the year. Maybe it was because of all the old growth trees or maybe it was because of the creek. "Shady" and "dripping" were two adjectives that came to mind when Zena thought about the Springs.

"Mr. Beaumont?" she called.

No answer.

"Hello. Is anybody here?"

No answer.

There was a certain protocol she followed. She didn't know if it was necessarily legal or not but she figured she could do pretty much anything within reason. Anything that wasn't completely out of line. She was not the landlord, after all. Merely the flaky art school graduate daughter, offering to pitch in and help in exchange for a free ride through life. Little more than an office assistant. Sounded good to her.

A rectangular black wooden table dominated the dining room. Probably a four- or, at best, six-seater. There were no chairs. A couple of dead plants cancerously blighted a wrought iron stand. The floor and everything else was gritty with dust.

She had not always been so brazen about entering the house. Her parents owned many houses throughout the town and surrounding farm country and this was the only one she would ever enter like this. She had been working for her parents since shortly after graduating a prestigious private art school in New England. The school was very similar to Twins Springs' own Shrine College, the place that, she guessed, really put it on the map. Shrine College was why many people knew the town of Twin Springs when there probably wasn't really any reason for them to.

That was ten years ago.

No one had rented this for more than thirteen months at a time. And it was always May to May. Which meant that it sat vacant for eleven months out of the year. It was something she and her parents never even really thought about anymore. Her father had drawn up a contract from May 1st one year through May 30th the following, the rent was twice what it was for any of their other properties, and it was always taken. Twin Springs was a highly sought after area. The school system was good. Crime was low. There were things to do and restaurants to eat in. It was a welcome liberal enclave in a mostly conservative part of the state. "For Sale" signs rarely lasted more than a month and she had placed rent signs in yards and turned around in an hour to remove them because the property had been taken that quickly. Now, with the internet, she barely needed to put out signs.

Not so with 523 Glowers.

Her father told her it had been like this for as long as he could remember. One year he'd put a sign in the yard that said FREE RENT with his phone number beneath it. He left it up for eleven months and didn't receive a single call. Until late April. Zena was too young to remember it but that was the year that writer guy had lived there. Holger Something-or-the-other. Twin Springs was an artsy, literate place. There were probably many people living here over the years who fancied themselves writers but this guy had actually had some stuff published. Zena couldn't remember any of the titles. It was trashy, Stephen King-type stuff she'd never really been interested in. The guy disappearing off the face of the planet without a trace didn't even make his name more known. JD Salinger was just a reclusive asshole and that only helped his popularity. Not poor Holger Writer Guy, though. Maybe it was just the difference between timeless literature and sensationalistic pulp. Hell, maybe it had been a pen name. When her father informed Holger the free rent only applied through April, he said the guy seemed unaware and offered to come in and pay all thirteen months up front.

So she knew, if it was beyond May 31st and she entered the house, she would be alone.

Only she never really felt alone.

At first she'd been terrified of finding someone dead but that hadn't happened either.

She was not aware of anyone dying in the house. So she hesitated to think the presence she felt was a ghost. It was probably just her imagination.

Now she stood in the library. That's what it looked like Alan Beaumont had used it for, anyway. Some people liked to use it for a study or guest bedroom. One family had even used it as the playroom. It had a large window in one wall and a door that let in as much light as the shady backyard would allow. The door opened to the back patio, if it could really be called that. It was a thing of bizarre . . . not beauty, exactly . . . Existence, maybe. She had no idea who created the patio but it looked like he'd had a bunch of spare bricks and got drunk with his friends while they placed them on the ground. The bricks mostly touched each other. It didn't look like any mortar had been used and they weren't at all even. While they may have been drunk when they laid the patio, she had to think that being drunk post-construction was a bad and possibly dangerous idea. So, yes, it was bizarre the patio even existed. Why spend time on something that looked like that? Why not scrap it and hire a professional?

A desk was pushed against the door. She would never know if it was so he could enjoy the view or if he was trying to keep something out. The window had what looked like a large dreamcatcher hanging from it with a sachet of something fastened to it. She sniffed the sachet. It smelled dry and dusty with maybe an underlying odor of rotting flowers.

She performed a quick survey of the bookshelves. Since no one had ever left behind anything like a computer or laptop or smart phone or even a diary, the bookshelves were often the best way to figure out what went on in some of these people's heads. Mr. Beaumont had seemed to like books on various religions with an emphasis on the occult. Or maybe those were the books he was least interested in. Maybe those were the ones he cared so little about that he left them behind.

She looked at his agreement again to see if it listed an occupation or an employer. She raised her eyebrows. It was like Mr. Beaumont knew his renting this house was in no way contingent to his employment.

EMPLOYER: FUCK ALL GODS
ADDRESS: 123 Anywhere Street
                Anyplace, Ohio 66666
PHONE: 1-800-BUTTSEX

She wondered if her parents kept any of the previous tenants' agreements on file. If so, it could make for some amusing reading.

In the middle of the room was a small, uncomfortable looking futon couch. Zena immediately thought of it as a bachelor's couch. There was a single book on the couch. It was called *The Book of Lies* by someone named Aleister Crowley. Zena thought the name sounded familiar although it carried a vaguely negative connotation. She thought about taking it since it seemed like this might possibly be the last thing Mr. Beaumont had read before he left. But she figured there would be plenty of time for that. If people didn't clean out this house before vacating it, they never came back for their stuff. Everything in here was now Zena's responsibility to get rid of. This had happened plenty of times before. Her parents had once tried to simply open the doors and have an estate sale, perfectly willing to let everything go for free, but no one showed up. Even when Zena listed shit on eBay, it sat there for an inordinately long time before selling. Nowadays, she was more inclined to pay junk men to just come and remove everything.

She left the library behind, moving back through the dining room and turning left into the narrow kitchen, making another left into the living room. More dust. A faint odor of incense. A couch. A couple of chairs. A low coffee table. A couple more dead plants. No television. No stereo. No DVDs or CDs or records. Not that there was any need for physical media anymore. All one needed was an internet connection to stream everything from space. She imagined every work of art that had ever been created orbiting the earth like an asteroid belt.

She walked through the living room, turned right into a short hallway, and entered the kitchen. She now looked through the kitchen and into the dining room. Sometimes different perspectives provided fresh insights to things. But she didn't have any revelations. She opened up some cabinets and drawers. All silverware, plates, and cups seemed to be left here. A coffeemaker and grinder were plugged into the wall but she was sure the power had been turned off, probably as of this morning. She opened the refrigerator, figuring she should probably remove any food that might have or would potentially go bad. There was a half-empty glass bottle of water with a rubber pop-top and an unopened bottle of Stone IPA. She'd probably take that back and put it in her own refrigerator.

The freezer contained three empty ice cube trays and a yellowed letter, still kind of cool to the touch, that read: REMEMBER TO GIVE BACK.

Cryptic, maybe. Or maybe just a simple reminder.

She walked down the hallway, stopping at the bathroom on the right just long enough to throw back the shower curtain and lift the toilet seat to make sure nothing too organic had been left behind. She'd have to remember to wash her hands when she got back to the office.

She glanced into the bedroom at the end of the hall but it was completely empty.

The smaller bedroom across the hallway contained a bed with messed up covers and a chest of drawers.

She wondered why Beaumont would have chosen the smaller bedroom and reminded herself he might not have been the only person living here, even though his was the only name on the agreement. Maybe he'd actually spent most of his nights in the larger bedroom and decided to take that stuff with him because it was newer or more expensive or more comfortable. Or maybe he had preferred this bedroom because of the large window looking out into the backyard and the thick woods beyond. It was a good view. There were no curtains hanging on the window and she wondered if Mr. Beaumont had ever put any up.

She watched two squirrels fucking in the yard. In the distance, a cat hunkered in the tall grass, hiding in the shadow of the woods, ready to spring into action.

In his closet she found that Mr. Beaumont preferred mostly khaki pants and blue jeans with a number of black shirts, one light blue oxford, and a clown costume. This was more creepy than hilarious and she tried to convince herself it was probably a Halloween costume. Still, she pulled it out and inspected it for blood, rips, anything. Nothing. Not really a surprise.

She went through the chest, expecting to find socks and underwear and t-shirts since most of the clothes seemed to be left behind. The only thing she found was an eight-inch black dildo in the middle drawer.

She closed the drawer, embarrassed.

Why was she embarrassed?

She didn't know. Now that she thought about it, it seemed irrational.

There's no one here with you.

You're all alone.

All alone.

With her hand on the dusty chest of drawers, she stared almost longingly into the woods across the yard. They seemed darker and more foreboding than the woods closer to town. A person could get lost in these woods.

The squirrels had finished fucking.

A third squirrel came up and began fucking the squirrel that had been on the bottom.

It made Zena think of a rabbity guy in a porno waiting his turn.

The cat sprang out from the woods and attacked the now idle squirrel.

All four animals made panicked squeals and dispersed.

There was an explosion of bird sounds. The birds were still there, watching.

Maybe it was all the animals making Zena feel watched.

But an animal was not a person. An animal could react to something she did, but it had no way of recounting her actions. Beyond the animals, there was the other natural world – the trees, the weeds, the sky – that never reacted to something a human did. Not consciously anyway. Not by choice.

Zena realized she was wet.

You're all alone.

She wondered if she was ever alone. Sometimes she felt like she had to do things to prove she was alone. To prove there was not always a reaction to her actions. To prove this to herself. This sensation of being watched was really just ego, she thought.

She slowly lay down on the bed, watching the early afternoon make the green backyard glow.

She shucked down her pants and underwear and ran her fingertips over herself, spreading her labia. The cat was back, spotting her, casually licking its paw. Not judging her. Zena scooted to the edge of the bed, her pants still around her ankles. The chest was close enough for her to reach forward and open the drawer, pull out the dildo.

She didn't know if it had been cleaned since its last use. She didn't know how many times or on how many people it had been used.

She didn't care.

She leaned back.

The cat was gone.

She stared at the ceiling and slowly slid the dildo inside of her, as deep as it would go. She looked at the shadows gathering in the corners of the room and closed her eyes and created a shadow within herself. When she thought about who she pictured on top of her, she wasn't surprised to think it was probably Alan Beaumont, even though she had no idea what he looked like. A stranger thought – that this was his big black mummified cock she had so deep inside her. That turned her on more than it disgusted her.

On the way out, she threw the dildo in one of the trashcans outside. It was now a talisman of her guilt. She hadn't used one of those in a really long time. She'd forgotten how pleasurable it could be. In many respects, it was the perfect man. The house was only a ten-minute walk from the office so she hadn't bothered driving. She walked slowly, as if in a daze.

She thought about stopping off at her house before going to the office. She should probably wash her hands and change her underwear.

CANDY HEART

In the middle of the woods, Diane Celine whirled around, her pulse quickening. Sudden movements snapped twigs around her. Her eyes stabbed the moonlit darkness, trying to find the source of the noise. Madness gnawed at her, the culmination of weeks of worry.

If she stopped to think about it, if she stopped to think why she was standing out here in the cold purplish darkness, beneath the bare trees and the fat moon, she could *almost* see the lunacy of her situation. Almost, but not quite. Maybe another month or two of fruitless searching and she would be there, ready to bow to sanity and run the opposite way . . . but not yet.

Joey was gone. Her madness wouldn't bring him back. She didn't know who would take a six-year-old boy but she had seen the news enough to know it happened all the time.

Yes, those things happened all the time, only the television glass always added just enough of a layer of fiction to them so her thin wall of safety remained. That wall was gone now. All the faceless psychopaths she had heard about on the television had finally found her. Actually, they had found *Joey*. And now she was prepared to do anything necessary to bring him back.

If something in her gut told her to leave the house and come out here to this clearing in the woods then that was exactly what she was going to do. If that gut feeling had told her to wake up and drink a pint of motor oil, she would have done that too. She didn't have to explain herself to anybody and if something happened, if one of those gut instincts panned out and she found Joey, the need for explanations would be erased.

Again, there were those scurrying sounds off in the woods, heavy and so *quick*. Her head whipped to the side, breath spuming out like factory steam.

Probably just a deer, she thought.

Then a pain ripped up her spine and she dropped to the floor of the woods.

The weeks had passed in a darkening whirlwind where some things, mental things – thoughts and memories – were smashed, shattered, or devoured completely.

It began with the morning she woke up and found Joey gone. His father had run out on them a long time ago and now it was just the boy and she, living alone in a ramshackle house between a winter quiet town and hibernating woods. Amazing how she could live alone like that and never have so much as an inkling of fear. Also amazing was how fast the fear could wrap its steel-thick trapjaws around her heart, lungs, and mind.

The day was off, not quite right, from the moment she woke up on the couch in the living room. It took her a couple of minutes to put things together. She was confused, unable to recall the last time she had fallen asleep anywhere except her bed. Maybe she had dropped off while watching television.

She searched her mind for an explanation.

The pills.

It had to be the pills.

She had changed doctors last week and the new doctor (she remembered jokingly referring to him as "the incredibly hairy Dr. Bath" to Joey) had changed her pills. He told her these new ones would still help her sleep at night when the red anxiety crawled all over her skin, but they wouldn't leave her feeling so groggy the next day. She wasn't used to them. That must be why she fell asleep on the couch. But she still couldn't see how that fully explained it. She always doubled up on the old pills during this most special time of the month because they helped with her cramping and bloating as well as her anxiety. Sometimes she thought the pills were like some magical cure all. Now if they could just take care of excess weight, depression, and a tight financial situation . . .

Not only had she passed out on the couch, she had also overslept. The angle of the meager February light coming in from the windows told her she should already be at work and Joey should already be at school.

With her heart pounding and her head in a foggy spin she started to run down the hall and wake Joey before something caught her eye.

Glass double doors faced the woods, taking up half of one wall in the living room. It provided a good view. It was one of the things that made her decide to rent this place upon walking into it, despite it being a little out of her price range. There was something smeared across the doors – a clear, hardened substance – something that reminded her of snot.

She stopped before turning into the dim hallway. A thought popped into her head, reaffirming her assertions that she *needed* the pills she took. She had to get rid of whatever that was on the doors. She would not be able to think of anything else until it was gone. She would yell at Joey and be tense all day at work if she knew that single streak of yuckiness was still there.

Rushing into the bathroom, she grabbed some paper towels and Windex, opened the double doors and vigorously cleaned the snotlike substance from them. The streak was about six inches wide and, at its arc, reached her chest. It made her think of a large drooly dog. Maybe a coyote, she thought, for she had heard them howling at night.

Once the streak was gone, she immediately felt a little more clearheaded, now able to go wake up Joey and get ready for work.

She glanced into her bedroom as she passed it and noticed a light flashing from her answering machine. A digital red "2" blinked repeatedly as she approached it.

Shit, she thought. The first was probably Joey's school, calling to find out where he was. The school would have probably called her work, also. The other message was probably from work.

Way to get everyone all worried, sleepyhead. How was she going to excuse Joey? Give him a note letting the teacher know that his mom was an anxiety-ridden pill popper?

She hit the play button and listened to the messages robotically spurt from the machine while she hurried to Joey's room, not knowing why she now felt so sure he wasn't going to be in his bed. Until that point, that pinprick of panic, she had simply thought he would be in there sleeping because she had not woken him.

Please let that feeling be wrong.

She saw a lump in the covers and her hopes rose until she reached the bed and punched down on the hollow fabric, feeling nothing, her heart beginning to steadily increase its rate.

She could only hope one of the messages was from Joey or somebody who could tell her he was safe and sound. It *was* perfectly possible he had woken up on his own, gotten dressed, and gone out to wait for the bus. But he just seemed too young for that.

Her feelings were right about the messages. One of them from Joey's school, one of them from work. Both of them sounded vaguely concerned but more concerned with her complete failure to call and report either of these absences than any kind of panicked, *genuine* concern like that which now surged through her body.

The alarm she felt held court with an overwhelming sense of guilt. The last time she had seen Joey, she had sent him to bed early because he had scattered little candy hearts she had bought for him on Valentine's Day around the house. She had been incredibly mad at him. Even after yelling at him about the mess, he had tried to smuggle some of the hearts into bed with him, the palm of his sweaty little hand multi-colored pastel after she pried them from it.

She spent the next hour searching the house inside and out, not finding anything.

He was gone. How could she have let this happen? Before letting panic punch a devastating hole in her sanity, she tried to seize on the only rational explanation.

His father had somehow found a way into the house and lured the boy away. He had been threatening to do that ever since the divorce three years ago and now she figured he probably had. A secret part of her, buried beneath the hate and resentment, almost *wanted* this to be the case. At least then she knew he would be safe, or as safe as a child could be in the company of a womanizing alcoholic.

Now she figured his father could probably make an actual case for gaining custody of Joey, coming into the house to find her whacked out of her skull on sleeping pills, completely neglecting Joey's education and her means for financial support. What would it matter that he had only before come to see Joey sporadically, at best? Or that he had paid her exactly nothing in child support?

She wanted to call the bum, but she just couldn't bring herself to do that. He would just lie to her or try to make her feel smaller than she already felt.

She did the only thing she could think was left to do. She called the police. Officer Branson was very kind to her. He asked all the right questions. He kept her calm. He asked her about her ex-husband, Stanley. Surprisingly, she was able to answer most of the officer's questions in a reasonably intelligent manner, even though it felt like her brain or her heart was going to swell and pop out of her body. Branson assured her they would contact the police in Stanley's area and have them check out the situation.

That afternoon, she called Officer Branson again, wanting

to know if they had any leads. Branson told her they had questioned Stanley and were not under the impression he had Joey. Stanley had let them come in and search his house without a warrant.

She had already known this. Stanley had called her as soon as the officers left, out of his head with anger and frustration. Of course he blamed her and she didn't think she had a right to disagree with him. He said he was going to search on his own before hanging up the phone.

That evening, the police came to her house, dusting for prints, looking for any evidence of a break-in. Other officers searched the woods, questioning the occupants of the houses located closest to hers.

The next day, Diane broadened her own search to the woods. As the investigation progressed, she went back there every day, mentally mapping the dead trees as landmarks so she wouldn't end up searching the same area over and over. Sometime during the second week, she found something that gave her both a sense of dread and a faint glimmer of hope.

She almost didn't notice it at first. It could have been any tiny piece of debris. It was the *color* that caught her eye. Bending to pick it up, she saw that it was a pastel green candy heart.

The inscription on the tiny heart said: MAYBE.

She knew it was stupid. She knew it meant no more than what the kings of holiday commercialization intended it to mean but, under these circumstances, it seemed to contain some kind of mystical prophecy, like a girl on a first date opening a fortune cookie that says, "You have found the love of your life."

Maybe, she thought. *Maybe he* is *out here.*

She continued to search the woods all through the bitter cold days. She didn't know what she was looking for and she didn't know how she would be able to deal with it if she actually came upon his dead body lying out there somewhere.

All of her searching led to nothing. Only more panic, more depression, more guilt, an increased feeling of doom.

Down on her knees in the woods, a month later, staring longingly at the pale moon, everything came back to her.

The new medicine wasn't working.

The old pills had kept this . . . this *changing* away. Images of this night the previous month flashed through her dulling mind, before what was human was completely devoured by what was animal. There was just enough human left to grasp those fleeting animal images and feelings.

She had locked herself outside because she felt strange and she hadn't felt that way since before Joey was born and she knew what feeling that way meant.

She had tried to get into the house, tried so desperately, beating her snout against the door until she finally found one flimsy enough to batter open.

Only she hadn't had to batter it open at all. It opened for her. And Joey stood on the other side, looking at her with a combination of awe and fear until he realized what was in front of him. He took off running for his room, screaming. She had dragged him out here. He had yelled for her to stop. And she had tried to communicate to him that his time had come.

Oh my God, she thought. Had she murdered her own son? But before she could answer herself, those thoughts were gone, surrendered to the animal thoughts, the ones that could only focus on hunger and scent and desire.

Jeff Branson didn't know what the hell he was seeing. He didn't know why this shit always happened to him. He guessed that was what he got for trying to be a responsible officer, a good cop.

He wasn't even on duty, but there was something about the Celine woman's case that had really gotten to him. He didn't have any children of his own but, if he did, he would want to know that, should one of them go missing, the law would do everything in its power to bring them back. Jeff had taken a very active interest in her. It probably didn't hurt that he was single and she was single and not at all bad looking. He reassured himself it was more than that. The FBI and the state police, though informed of the disappearance, didn't really seem to be doing a damned thing about it. Diane had called him and told him about the clue, the little candy heart, and that had given him renewed desire to search for the boy.

Every chance he got, he had come out here to the woods behind the house. He didn't think it would hurt anything to wander around in the woods with his shotgun. If another clue didn't turn up then he figured that, at the very least, he might be able to bag a deer. Part of him wanted to tell the woman the boy was gone, that he probably would not be seen again. That was what his gut told him. It seemed like he had been through this too many times before. Not here, of course. Things like this didn't happen in Twin Springs, Ohio. But, fresh out of the academy, he had served on the Orlando force for three years. That had been enough for him. He couldn't find any comfortable resolution with the little children like he could manage with teenagers. Teenagers had ways of taking care of themselves. Some of them just ran off. Some of them were mixed up in really weird shit. Children did not just run off. They were usually taken. And the people taking them usually did not have wholesome goals in mind.

So tonight he had put on his plain clothes, his heavy winter jacket, grabbed his shotgun from his house, and come out here to wait. Maybe he had heard too many horror stories but he had visions of some crazy, child-abducting family living out here in the woods. They were probably cannibals, to boot. He knew there were a few communes on the surrounding farms. While many people saw this as a nearly Utopian attempt at peaceful coexistence, he could only think of the Manson family and cults. And he was hoping to catch one of them passing back and forth here in the deep night hours, thinking they were operating in complete secrecy.

Branson was more than a little surprised when he saw Diane stumble into the woods. He was going to approach her until he noticed she acted differently than the woman who had presented herself in front of him before. She seemed, not so much hysterical, as *wild*. He decided to watch and see what she was going to do, where she was going to go.

Suddenly, she stopped in the clearing and fell to her knees. He would have dismissed what happened next as complete fiction if he wasn't observing it firsthand.

The woman grew large. Hair sprouted out all over her body.

A werewolf, Branson thought, wanting to dismiss the idea as ludicrous as soon as it popped into his head.

But it was hard to dismiss as ludicrous when he could stand there and watch the face reach out into a snout, the teeth elongate and yellow, the ears grow and bend back, the clothes rip and fall away, the legs and arms deform, lowering the woman. He'd seen this occur in a number of horror movies and had always wondered why the person just stood around and watched this transformation happen. It never went quickly. Why didn't they just plug them? He figured it was just one of those movie anomalies, something that had to happen and shouldn't be thought about too much. But here he was thinking about it. Hell, here he was *doing* it. And he had the answer. Because a werewolf is not just a monster. It's almost always a person the watcher knows. And maybe they know that person as a decent person. It wasn't like the movies where the good guy hunts down the serial killer and stands paralyzed while the psycho soliloquizes.

Now fully formed, Diane sniffed at the ground, looking hungrily up at the moon. Branson crouched down but it didn't matter. She had already seen him. The doglike thing turned its head in his direction and growled, baring those sharp yellow teeth.

Now that it was a matter of self-defense, Branson took aim with the rifle and fired as the wolf lunged across the clearing at him. He doubted his bullets were silver and wondered if that even mattered.

He pressed the trigger again and again. The first shotgun blast sheared off the wolf's right front paw. The second blast took off a hunk of the snout, collapsing the thing. After the second shot, the gun only clicked as Branson pulled the trigger. Empty. He stayed where he was, just slightly occluded behind the bare shrubs.

The body of the wolf slowly turned back into the Celine woman. Branson felt like this would probably spell his end as a police officer. It was frowned upon to kill the people who you were trying to help. He felt certain he would eventually have to draw someone's attention to this naked, shot-up body that happened to belong to a woman he had somewhat openly taken a "special interest" in.

Another sound from the far end of the clearing.

What now? Branson thought.

Then he saw Joey. At least, he thought it *had* to be Joey. It was a smaller wolf than the one he had just shot and even though it was completely animal there was something about it that made Branson think of all those pictures Diane had shown him prior to the search. It was like watching a cartoon where the animated character vaguely resembles the actor doing the voiceover. The wolf strolled out into the clearing, approaching the body on the ground. It licked at the woman, nuzzling its wet nose against her neck and Branson swore he heard a whimper that sounded very much like a human cry.

The wolf looked into the woods where Branson crouched and issued a growl. Then it came at him. He couldn't load his gun fast enough. The wolf threw itself on Branson, its jaws gnashing in front of his face and Branson smelled, just faintly, the sugary smell of candy hearts. He wanted to laugh with the absurdity of it all but sharp teeth tore through his jugular and he was pretty sure he would never laugh again.

RUNNING FROM THE ROSES

The old woman lay on the bed, arms against her sides, eyes and mouth closed. Chloe thought her grandmother must be the only person who looked severe even when sleeping. Countless times Chloe had stood beside this bed, staring down at the old woman, waiting for the cessation of the covers' rising and falling. A part of Chloe looked forward to this. When she wasn't staring at the woman, she stared at the wallpaper, crawling with green vines and red roses. She didn't want to seem cruel and even though, in her grandmother's better days, the two women had fought continuously, Chloe didn't want to think she hated the woman.

She didn't want to think she was doing any of this out of hate.

Hate was the furthest thing from her mind. What she thought about on this sad day was love. It was her intense love for a boy named Jack Kettering that rooted the decisions of which the seeds had been planted much earlier.

Jack was on his way. Together, they were going to go to California and leave Twin Springs, Ohio, behind.

Her meager suitcase sat beside the front door inside the ramshackle house.

She stood over the bed, looking down at Grandma Elly and wishing things could have turned out differently. It was late summer and Chloe wore a black skirt that cut off just below the knee. Wind came in from the windows, touching her pale legs under the skirt and above her combat boots, making her feel amazingly alive in this, the most depressing stage of her life.

But she was young. Wasn't it okay to feel alive? Shouldn't she feel like the world was hers, spread out before her?

She pulled the uncomfortable wooden chair from in front of the wall over to the bed. She sat down and crossed her legs, leaning toward her grandmother.

The wind whistled as it was cut to pieces by the screens in the western windows.

"I won't leave if you just say something. Anything at all, Grandma."

But she knew the old woman wouldn't say anything.

Chloe felt feverish. Cold sweat stood out on her skin. What *should* she be feeling? She didn't know. She was only seventeen and nobody had ever sat her down and explained to her how one feels when confronted with this type of thing. She was too young to remember her parents dying. And that was different anyway. They were not the ones who had raised her. Who had loved her through everything since she was a baby. They were not the ones who had made her life a living hell for the past two years. And the only mystery they had left her with was the mystery of who they were and what they were like. She didn't expect them to be anything *but* mystery.

But her grandma *shouldn't* have been a mystery. Chloe wasn't an idiot when it came to human nature. Her grandma should have been an open book to her but she knew there were things about her grandma she didn't know about. Dark things. Maybe even scary things.

Off in the distance, the faint rumble of thunder rolled out of the hills.

"Jack's gonna be here soon, Grandma. I'm gonna go with him. Do you want me to go with him? Because I'll stay if you need me."

And she knew the old woman needed her. Of course she needed her. Chloe was the one who fed her. The one who changed her bedpan. The one who made sure a nurse came over once a week to check on her. She was also the one who made sure her grandma wasn't put in a home because that had been her last wish before lapsing into whatever complacent vegetable state she had lapsed into. Chloe knew it wasn't just pride keeping her out of the home. It was something else. It was that secret.

The sky darkened, throwing shadows across the room.

Chloe stood up from the chair and paced around the room, the room with the busy wallpaper that reflected a simpler time, a time when painted roses could almost pass for the real thing.

"You know, this hasn't been easy for me!" she screamed, knowing she didn't have to. She had screamed countless times before. It didn't matter whether her grandmother heard her or not. She wasn't going to respond. Nothing was going to make her respond. She wasn't screaming at her grand-mother anyway. Not really. She screamed because she felt like she had to. It kept the madness at bay.

The sky darkened further. The room dimmed along with it, the deep red roses of the wallpaper turning almost black. She imagined fat, malignant tumors covering the wall, held together by vines that were actually thick tendons, metastatic tendons carrying the malignancy from one tumor to the next.

"What's wrong with you, Grandma? You know I can't take it anymore, don't you? Why didn't you just let me put you in a home? Is it because they would run too many tests on you? Is it because they could take samples of your blood, samples of your skin and find out what you really are?"

She surprised herself with this last thing she said. It was the first time she had allowed that thought to be spoken aloud.

Growing up, it had never crossed her mind that her grandma was something else, something other than human. Something called, around town, a Zwinn. The Zwinns were myth, legend, scapegoats for the unexplained. Vampires, maybe. Maybe witches. Near demonic familiars that some-how took the place of their human counterparts. It made sense, now that she thought about it. It made even more sense when spoken aloud. Until then, she didn't think she believed in the Zwinns. She certainly didn't actually think her grandmother might *be* one. Chloe's idea was not unfounded. She was able to recall the genesis of that idea perfectly and, thinking back on it, was surprised it had taken her this long to give voice to her suspicions.

She had been young. Eight or nine. She woke up in her bedroom, the remnants of a terrible dream squirming through her head. She still remembered the dream vividly. She and her grandmother were running through the woods. It was dark. The moon hung full overhead only it wasn't the moon at all but the pale waxy face of a man. A terrifying man who struck some chord of familiarity within her. It was a face she would never forget and hadn't seen since but, nevertheless, she had often found herself wondering just who it was. Scared, she had wandered out of her bedroom. She heard voices coming from down the hall and figured her grandma must be out there watching television. She hadn't even thought her grandmother might have visitors because no one ever visited this sad old house unless it was one of her friend's parents coming to pick her up for a sleepover.

First checking the family room and finding it empty, she then went into the kitchen.

She squinted her eyes against the blue fluorescent glare of the light. The light seemed comforting at night when it was her and her grandma in there baking cookies or eating dinner, but now it just seemed harsh. Harsh and obtrusive. Obtrusive because there were people standing in the kitchen and the brightness of the light prevented Chloe from really focusing on them. There were three of them. Chloe moved a little closer, her eyes gradually adjusting to the light, able to make the figures out a little better. Two men and a woman. One of the men spotted her and flashed her a wan, secretive smile but didn't say anything. Didn't hint to her grandmother they were being spied on. And didn't that face look familiar? Wasn't it the face she had just seen in the moon, in her nightmare? Now it didn't seem so terrifying just . . . familiar. Where had she seen that face before?

The woman was the most beautiful woman Chloe had ever seen. She wore a very black, almost floor-length dress. Chloe couldn't identify the fabric in this lighting. Her black hair was pulled away from her face, high cheekbones, large eyes, large red lips. She was fashion magazine beautiful, Chloe thought. Now able to focus perfectly, she noticed the woman's eyes and, even from this distance, she could see the woman's green eyes sparkling – green bordering on yellow like some undiscovered gem.

Everyone in the kitchen whispered. At least Chloe thought they were whispering. They may not have been speaking at all. Chloe imagined a telepathic communication. Chloe's grandma was the only one who sat. She sat in a kitchen chair and had her right arm raised. The beautiful woman held her hand in both of hers. Chloe thought the woman held her grandmother's arm like a bottle of precious wine. She didn't know why she thought it but she wondered if these three people hadn't just been drinking from her grandma's arm.

It was a strange picture, a strange thought, but it was one that would come back to her many times over the years and it was the last night she remembered her grandma in quite that way because, seeing the older woman there in the chair, with her hand raised, was the last time she would think her grandma was being honest with her. There was a rift. It went unspoken but it was felt and that lack of verbalization only seemed to make it grow deeper.

Once her grandma knew she was standing there, she was quickly shooed to bed and, every day since then, Chloe had known the woman was keeping something from her. Something secret. Something Chloe desperately wanted to know. And there were times when Chloe would catch her grandmother staring at her and wondered if the old lady was reading her mind. That would certainly explain why she always managed to be a step ahead during their arguments.

That was the only time she had seen the strange people come to the old sad house but she knew they had come on different occasions throughout the years. She knew this because, when they visited, her grandma's physical condition deteriorated at an alarming rate. She couldn't help but think her grandmother was being bled dry. Bled dry by this triumvirate of mysterious people she had seen gathered in the kitchen that one night. But why? That, she didn't know. Perhaps her grandmother's life was precious to these people and slowly, slowly, they were sucking away the last of it. And then, two years ago, it had happened. Her grandma had gone from a woman of sixty-five to a woman who was on her deathbed.

And on her deathbed she had stayed.

Now, as the first of the rain started to water down on the house and all the huge trees around it, she sat on the side of the bed, wrapped in that clean linen scent, placing a hand on her grandmother's sallow chest.

"I think I know what they were, Grandma. But I want to know *who* they were. I want to know you didn't have a chance before I do this. I want to know I'm not helping to end any sort of life at all."

Thunder cracked outside. A gust of air, almost cold, swept into the room. The meager sunlight caught on the rain beading the window and added it to the already busy wallpaper. Now there were a lot of little gray tumors to go with the fat black tumor roses.

"Jack's going to be here soon, Grandma. Give me something. *Please.*"

Still, the old woman said nothing.

Thunder cracked again. The blazing glow of the lightning popped into the room for a split second. It was like an x-ray and, when she looked at her grandmother, the only thing she saw beneath the skin was dust.

From outside, she heard a car horn. Jack. Beautiful Jack, come to take her away.

She reached into the waistband of her skirt and pulled out the handgun. She didn't know much about guns. She didn't know what kind of gun it was. She didn't even know the name brand. She had fired it exactly once, into an old board out behind the house, to make sure it worked. It did. Not only did it work, it looked like it left a big enough hole to properly cremate a potential suicide's brains.

She held the gun over her grandma's nightstand.

"This is for when you wake up and realize I'm not here."

The *clunk* the gun made against the wood of the nightstand was as lethal sounding as the actual report the gun had made going off out behind the house.

"I'm sorry," Chloe said, the words sounding weak as they came out of her mouth. From all around her, the roses like tumors or hungry mouths seemed to wriggle across the walls. Breathing. Whispering her name. Begging her to stay.

She turned her back on her grandmother, turned her back on the hideous hungry roses, and left the house.

The storm raged down, spitting at her, and there was some deeply rooted religious part of her hoping God was not going to strike her down for what she had just done. She opened the passenger door of Jack's ancient Volvo and threw her suitcase in the backseat.

"Is everything okay?" Jack asked her when she slid into the passenger seat.

"No," she said, tears trying to claw their way out of her eyes. "But I knew it wouldn't be."

"We don't have to go," he said.

"Yes, we do. And you can't let me come back here, Jack. *Ever*. Do you promise?"

"Sure. I promise."

With that, they pulled away from the house, Jack commenting on the uselessness of his windshield wipers, talking about how he should have been better prepared. Chloe barely heard him.

He drove the first leg of the trip. She sat in the passenger seat with her eyes closed, feigning sleep in order to avoid conversation. She was much too sad and sick and confused to really fall asleep or to open her eyes and talk, for that matter.

She pretended to wake up just before midnight and they pulled into a rest stop somewhere in eastern Illinois. Jack said he was tired. She told him she would do some of the driving. They fucked in the passenger seat, Chloe straddling him. It was quick and furious. She was barely aroused and it was nearly painful but, for some reason, she had wanted to feel the solidity of Jack inside her, hot and real, stabbing her insides while his arms wrapped around her. Ever since she had met him, it was always this gesture that made her think things just might turn out all right.

She sat in the passenger seat with his come leaking out and into her ass crack. He put his big, warm hand on her knee and said, "What's the real problem?"

"I don't know," she said. She was crying again.

"You can tell me everything, you know? That's what this is really all about. That's why we're going away together. It's kind of like a marriage. Anything that bothers you, I want it to bother me too."

"You'd think I was crazy."

"We're from Ohio, remember? Crazy is relative. Actually, it's most of our relatives that are crazy."

Without expecting it, without really wanting to, she launched into the whole story. She told him everything. He didn't seem as concerned about the crazy supernatural stuff as he was about the gun she had left at her grandmother's bedside.

"If there's a gun involved, they'll come looking for us. You know that, don't you?"

"Well . . ." She tried to justify herself. "She said she didn't want to go into a home. I figured that, in the off chance she actually woke up and was somewhat aware of herself, she could, you know . . ."

"Chloe, this is the kind of thing the news gets ahold of and . . . and then we're finished. Then we have to come back and God only knows what happens after that."

"Maybe it was stupid," she said.

"No, no, we can fix it. We're not that far away."

"No, Jack. We can't go back. We can't. Nobody's going to come looking for us. It'll look like suicide."

"The gun's gonna have your prints on it. If she wakes up and does away with herself, you're going to look bad either way. You're either going to look like you abandoned her and were too gutless to call an ambulance or you're going to look like you shot her so you could get away and live your teenage life."

"No. It wasn't like that at all. I just didn't want anyone to find out about her."

"I know that. But think of how crazy that's going to sound to anyone else."

"And when we go back and find that nothing's happened . . . what then? We can't take her to a home. Then they'll know. Then they'll all know. And we can't live there with her."

"Why not?"

"Because I just can't. What we have . . . it's beautiful. I don't want it mixed up with that. I want to make a clean beginning."

"Well, maybe we'll have to wait until she's gone before we make our beginning. I don't mind, Chloe, really I don't. I'd do anything for you."

"I know you would. That's what makes me so scared."

"Forget about all that Zwinns stuff. It's all just rumors and lies."

"Okay. We can go back. But if we go back, we're getting someone to take care of her. Are you willing to work enough to support that?"

"I'm willing to do anything you ask me to do."

"Who's driving?" she asked, turning petulantly in her seat and reaching in the floorboard for her underwear.

"I'll drive," he said.

"Let's get this over with then."

Jack drove. She watched the rain beat against the windshield and she couldn't think of anything except the wallpaper in her grandmother's room. She didn't know why she thought of it. Maybe she thought of it in order to take her mind off all the other things she could have been thinking about. Maybe it was the intricate pattern of the wallpaper that kept her mind busy, tracing it over and over. No. Not *it*. The *memory* of it. And she still thought of the roses as tumors and the raindrops as little baby tumors but, after a bit of driving, she saw the tumors clearing up. Like they were going away. Mouths closing, satiated. Memories were tricky things.

Something inside her told her that her grandmother was better now. Another part of her told her this was insanity and, even if that was the case, then maybe it was Chloe who had made her sick these last couple of years. Maybe her being gone was the best thing to happen to her grandma. Or maybe it just meant things would work out. Things would be different. If she had Jack there to help her with her grandma, maybe things wouldn't be so bad. Or if they put her grandma in a home. Really, what was stopping them from doing that? The Zwinns weren't real. Just like Jack said. They were made up. They were a scapegoat for what ailed the town. *Reality* was what really ailed the town.

In her mind, she saw the wallpaper in a sunny room. All the tumors were gone and now it was just the roses, dark red with deep green vines against an off-white background. Normal roses. Normal wallpaper. A normal life. The way it should be. It wouldn't be the ideal beginning but Chloe thought, maybe, it was the only way she could be truly happy—to have both people who mattered near her at all times.

The trip back seemed to go a lot quicker than their abbreviated trip toward their nonexistent California dreamland. Sometime before dawn, they reached the sad old house nestled at the edge of the woods, surrounded by towering trees.

"I guess we're here," Jack said.

"Yeah," Chloe said. She didn't want to go inside but knew she had to. Going inside, coming back, that was doing the right thing. She didn't know what she had been thinking. She wasn't that type of person. The type of person who leaves a dying old woman in bed with a gun to off herself if she came to and found herself alone. Jack wasn't that type of person. Of course, she had never told Jack about the gun until they were at the rest stop. She had told Jack someone would be there to look after her grandmother. Now they were back and that was that. That was doing the right thing. It felt good.

"I guess I should go in," she said.

"I'll come with you."

"No," she said. "I mean, I think I should go in alone. I don't want you to see anything you shouldn't see. This is my mess."

"Are you sure? I want to. I mean, I wouldn't mind."

"Yeah, I'm sure. You stay here. Let me make sure everything's okay. I'll come back out. I still don't know what I'm going to do."

"Just don't do anything stupid."

"You mean like use the gun myself . . . on her, just to put an end to it?"

"That's exactly what I mean."

"I couldn't do that."

"I know you couldn't . . . wouldn't . . . Okay, I'll be here. If you're gone too long, I'm coming in to check on you though."

"'Kay."

Then they kissed and she didn't want to release his lips. The second she pulled away from him, she felt an overwhelming sense of emptiness. The time for hesitation was over. She had to do this. She had to go back in. This could be a beginning too, she realized, even if maybe it wasn't the beginning she had originally wanted.

The door creaked open. The house was dark and scary. She couldn't remember a time she had ever been scared in this house. The night she had seen the strangers, that didn't even make her scared. It filled her with something else. Something like wonder and awe. But what she felt now was fear and she didn't know why she felt that way.

She flipped on a light as soon as she found it, hoping it would chase some of the scariness away.

The light came on, spreading through the hallway like a beacon to her grandmother's bedroom door. Even though she had only been gone for a few hours, the house looked different. It looked and felt even sadder and she didn't know why she had come back. Coming back was perhaps the stupidest thing she had ever done, she now realized. They couldn't do this. She and Jack would not be able to live in this house with that woman down the hall. Of that, she was certain.

She walked down the hallway, wanting to get it over with, wanting to confront those crazy fears raping her mind. She wanted to get to the end of the hallway and go to her grandmother's bedroom and see that the woman was just as wooden and dormant as always and then she could call the ambulance and they would come and take her away because even if they took her in and ran tests on her they weren't going to find anything, were they? Of course they weren't. Because the Zwinns didn't exist. They were myth. They were legend. They couldn't be part of her.

Chloe flung the door open and her heart stopped for just a second.

The old woman was not on the bed.

The first thought she had was that the roses had climbed down off the walls, *grown* down off the walls and covered the bed, ate her grandma with their hungry mouths or ultra rapid cancer. Then her heart sped up. Of course those weren't roses.

They were bloodstains.

Her grandmother had woken up and found the gun. The gun lay in the middle of the bed, covered in those vulgar, drippy-looking roses.

But where was her grandmother?

Had there been time for the ambulance to come and find her? Had she called them before doing it?

Her heart doubled its pace.

She had to get out of here. She had to get out of this carnage. She didn't even care about answers anymore. She just wanted to grab Jack and then they could go off and do what they had planned. What they had wanted to do for so long now.

But the door was blocked.

Her grandmother stood in the doorway, flanked by two of the people she had seen in the kitchen the one night. Her grandmother's long gray hair was down, falling around her shoulders in bloody clumps. Her mouth was blackened. Chloe gagged, went down on her knees, staring at the atrocities in the doorway. To her grandmother's right was the beautiful woman. To her left was the man whose face Chloe had seen in the moon.

In that instant, she understood everything, knowledge as ubiquitous as the coppery blood smell around her.

"Why didn't you tell me?" she mumbled through a mouth gone cotton.

"Thank you for making me free," Chloe's grandma said, approaching her.

"Stay away!" Chloe spat.

She knew who the people with her grandmother were. Those were Chloe's parents. She was surprised she didn't notice the resemblance that night in the kitchen. And it was true, they had died in an accident but they had become something else. Something that fed off the living. Something nightmares were made of. And her grandmother had lived so that she could feed them only, eventually, the old woman had dried up. Her parents looked gaunt, wasted.

Chloe knew exactly what they wanted of her. Maybe she would just grab the gun and explode her head and give them what they wanted, give them the blood, give them the life. In her mind, she mapped where the gun lay on the bed. She needed to have it in her hand only she didn't know whom she was going to use it on.

Her grandmother stayed out of Chloe's reach but continued to talk.

"I'm glad all the secrets are out. Now we can be like a family again. There's nothing we can do to help it."

"I'm not going to be like you," Chloe said. "I'm not going to turn myself into a wasted wreck so you can continue being whatever you are."

"There's nothing you can do to stop it," her mother said.

"The fuck I can't," Chloe said.

She sprang up to her feet and grabbed the gun, putting it to her temple.

"Chloe, no!" Jack shouted from the doorway, shoving her family aside and flinging himself on her.

He grabbed her wrist and yanked the gun away from her head. But Chloe was not going to let him stop her. She pulled the trigger and the gun went off with a deafening explosion.

Chloe never felt the impact.

She reeled back on the bed and looked around her. Jack stood at the foot of the bed, the top right half of his head blown away. But he didn't drop. He didn't go down.

She wondered why it had taken her until now to recognize him for who he was. He had been in the kitchen that night also. Maybe it was the way the dawn slanted in through the window, reflecting off all the roses scattered across the bed and the floor and Chloe's arms.

The roses were hungry.

She knew that, no matter how many bullets she decided to put into Jack, in any of them for that matter, they would not die. Because they were already dead. Or, perhaps, beyond death. So, doing what she had originally planned, she put the gun to her head and pulled the trigger but the gun didn't fire. She tried again and again – nothing and nothing. Jack approached her, removed the gun from her hand. She thought about struggling but didn't know what value struggling would have. Jack had been the dream, or at least part of the dream, and now he was part of the nightmare. He pushed her back on the bed. She extended her arms out to either side and, with deathbright eyes, the Zwinns tore her open and fed from the blood coursing through her veins.

Chloe thought about a little girl she had seen downtown the other day. Perhaps she could take that girl. Take her and call her her daughter. Bring her here, tell her lies the entire time she grew up. Maybe she would even tell her about the roses on the wall. Tell her they were really like tumors . . . or hungry mouths. Tell her they would consume everything she knew and loved. Or maybe Chloe would just tell her to run. To run and run until she was so far away from this place it was just a distant memory. And, if the girl ever saw any strange visitors, Chloe could tuck her into bed and tell her it was nothing. Really, it was nothing. Just a bad dream. Just a nightmare. And everybody knows nightmares end when we open our eyes.

THE MAN WHO HATED STEPHEN KING

Mariska found herself in the small town of Twin Springs. It had happened more than a few times in the nearly three decades since the disappearance of her father. And why not? It was a quaint town. Charming. It was someplace that would seem almost at home in a Bradbury story. Maybe even a Stephen King story. Hell, maybe that was even more appropriate. There was more a sense of '60s counterculture and baby boomers living out their golden years than Norman Rockwell American pie-ism, now that she thought about it. But that name – Stephen King – she didn't like to think about it. She'd never read one of his books and probably never would. She wasn't really much of a reader anyway. Her father had hated Stephen King far more passionately than he hated most things.

She had come to Twin Springs for the fall street fair but had apparently missed it by a week. She wasn't really sure how that had happened. The town was currently no busier than it was on any other gorgeous Saturday in early October and signs for the fair were still posted here and there.

She paid for her small black coffee at the tiny, dirty café and contemplated dropping into the used bookstore next to it, but that made her gag a little. The only reason she would have gone in was to see if they had any of her father's books on the shelf. She wondered if bookstores still even had horror sections. Then she remembered that this particular bookstore – Thing Books, here for as long as she could remember – had called it 'terror,' not horror. Her father had dragged her in here countless times and then he'd stopped. In retrospect, he'd probably been banned. He had a tendency to be goading and cantankerous, especially when he left the house.

She pulled her knit cap down over her ears, extracted her electronic cigarette from her coat pocket and took a long and satisfying hit. Not as satisfying as the real thing, she was sure, but using it made her feel less like an addict.

Addiction was a family curse.

An older couple passed her and said 'hi.' She nodded and tried her best to smile. She moved in the direction of the state park and it didn't occur to her what she was doing until she stood at the trailhead taking a warming sip of her coffee, another hit from her fake cigarette, and staring at the beauty of leaves that had not yet dropped.

She was subconsciously moving in the opposite direction of *the house*. The house where her father had disappeared from on a bitter cold winter night nearly thirty years ago. Although she always had to wonder if he'd disappeared *from* the house or *into* the house.

It was a ridiculous thought, she knew.

She decided to catch the last hour or so of daylight and drift into the woods. She told herself these were not the same woods looming behind that house. After all, there was the whole town separating them. But they probably wrapped around. They probably *were* the same woods.

But they didn't feel the same. These were somehow thinner, sparser. They let more of the good sunlight through.

Maybe there were fewer pines or something. Maybe they just grew from soil that wasn't blighted and cursed.

Now Mariska found herself wanting something even stronger than an actual tobacco cigarette. Maybe a joint. She didn't even know where that thought came from. She'd never really liked pot and the last time she'd smoked it was probably five years ago when she had dated a guy roughly the same age she was now. He'd been going through something of a mid-life crisis. He smoked pot, listened to Nirvana on vinyl, and wore old school Doc Martens. After she dumped him she'd referred to him as Mr. Nineties around her friends.

She wandered deeper into the woods until she came to the town's namesake, Twin Springs. It was an odd name she guessed, since it really appeared to be one creek. Enough so that a lot of people referred to it as Twin Springs Creek, which seemed somehow redundant. Maybe, somewhere, there were two springs joining to form this creek. She didn't know. She wasn't much on research. Sometimes knowing the way things worked destroyed the mystery. She preferred to look at the single creek rushing through the gorge and imagine the interplay between two streams of water. Two things with completely different origins combining into one seamless whole.

She breathed the late afternoon air, crisp, full of clean water, damp bark, and earth.

If she was going to go by the house – and she knew she would – she needed the fortification.

She finished off her coffee and chucked the cup off the ledge and into the creek.

Holger Blackwell bought all of Stephen King's books as they came out, read them, and burned them. Tonight's offering was going to be *It*. It was a good night for it. For *It*. Early February and the fire looked hungry.

Her father had seemed to be in a bad mood all night. He'd sat in his shabby chair and chuffed his way through the last few pages of the book while Mariska sat in front of the television and watched *Strawberry Shortcake*. She knew she was lucky to have a VCR. She was the only one of her friends at school who had one. Of course, she only had one here, at her dad's. Her mom liked to say her dad used it as a babysitter but her mom liked to make everything her dad did sound bad. In retrospect, Mariska realized the only reason she was probably able to come to her dad's was because her mom wanted to go on dates or maybe just have the night alone.

Holger closed the book and placed it on the coffee table.

"Why's it so big?" Mariska's books were a fraction of this size.

"Who knows? It could have probably been half that long."

Holger's latest book, the one that would turn out to be his last, was called *The Jackthief*, and it was nearly as long. Only his book had only ever been a Tor paperback so it didn't have the mass of King's hardcover. And it was only so bulky because the print and spacing were larger. *The Jackthief* had never even been picked up by the Book of the Month Club so it would, alas, never see a hardcover release, not even a poorly printed, not-quite-full-size shabby one. And, technically, it wasn't his *final* book, but it was the last one published while he was alive. Mariska's mother had unearthed a partially finished manuscript of a book called *The One Who Creeps* and bestowed it upon Mariska because, well, Holger didn't have anything else to leave behind. Mariska had never read it, had never read any of her father's books. It seemed weird and invasive and she was pretty sure it would end up making her dislike him. An odd man named Gregory Seymour had contacted her when she was in her mid-twenties, asking her about her dad's books, which had all gone out of print. He said he'd like to do limited editions of them and she said, "Tell me where to sign." The partial manuscript of *The One Who Creeps* came up and Seymour said he knew a really good author who could do a bang up job of completing it. Mariska didn't even ask who it was, just said, "Yeah, sure," and asked how much this gig paid. Seymour said he was struggling, the whole book industry was doing poorly, and the most he could offer at this time was five thousand dollars. The contract arrived two days later along with the check. Mariska signed away the rights to all of Holger's books, put the contract on top of the partial manuscript, put it all in a large bubble mailer and washed her hands of the whole writing business. She was young, after all, and five thousand dollars could be a decent down payment on a house or nearly a year's worth of rent. That wasn't exactly what it went for, but it did allow her to have a really exciting, if not completely memorable, few months.

Mariska sat on her knees in front of the coffee table, rubbing the glossy back cover of the book.

"Is he a rock star, too?" she asked. "Is that why he's playing the guitar?"

"He's playing the guitar because he wants you to know

he's rich enough to indulge any interest he has."

"Is that bad?"

"I don't know."

Holger rarely spoke to Mariska like a child so she only grasped a little of what he meant. Maybe he was hoping she would remember what he said and the meaning would color itself in as she got older. Maybe that had been the case.

He picked the book back up, riffled the pages and made an exasperated sigh. He looked exhausted. He only ever wore black. Tonight he wore a thick black sweater over his customary black work shirt and corduroys. This made his whiskered chin, the circles under his eyes, and the lines in his face look even darker than they actually were.

"What happened to his beard?" she asked. "I liked his beard."

"He's all yuppified now. You want to look like your target audience and those college hippies have all grown up."

"Are yuppies bad people?"

"They're monsters."

An author photo of Holger Blackwell had never appeared in or on one of his books. Mariska had once thought maybe it was because there wasn't anyone to take one, then she'd thought her dad just didn't want an author photo or that if someone saw a photo of him they wouldn't buy the book. Her dad looked scary. She didn't think that at the time, but looking back through her mother's photo albums at the younger Holger Blackwell – always in black, never smiling, looking at the person holding the camera like he wanted to eat them – she thought maybe that was the case. That notion didn't drop until she got older and realized the world – especially women – loved evil men.

Holger stood up and opened the door to the fireplace. This was at least the third such offering she'd witnessed.

"Mom says it's wrong to burn books."

"I'm the child of Nazis," Holger said and chucked the book into the fire.

Mariska paused her video and stood watching the fire, taking her father's pinky finger in her little hand.

One thing Mariska had learned was that books didn't really burn well. They curled up at the edges. They blackened. Her father had to jab it with the poker several times and Mariska had completely lost interest and gone back to *Strawberry Shortcake* before it completed its transformation into ash.

Holger placed the poker back in its stand, closed the fireplace door, dusted his hands, and said, "Well, it's time to get back to work."

A period of furious activity usually followed one of the burnings. It never really occurred to Mariska that when her father left her there in front of the television, when he went through the kitchen and the dining room and into his office, that he was sitting at his desk to work on *The One Who Creeps*.

She fell asleep on the floor in front of the television.

She dreamed she was outside, in the woods behind the house. She was freezing cold. The woods around her were frozen but the leaves were still on the trees. They were frosted over with ice and it made her think of a moth's wings. She could sense someplace warm and moved toward it. A stabbing wind rolled through the woods and the frozen trees creaked and moaned like they'd been frozen forever. She reached what she thought was the back door to her house but when she got closer to it she realized it was the door to a giant fireplace and assumed this was the warm place she sought. Drawing even closer, she saw her father beside the door. Children were lined up behind him and he casually plucked the first in line and tossed it into the house, into the roaring fire. He spotted Mariska and a bolt of fear seized her. Her father said in a voice that didn't sound at all like his own, "Don't be afraid. Take your place at the back of the line." She obediently did so. She thought it would be awful, standing at the back of the line and waiting her turn to be burned alive, even though, at this rate, it looked like it would take her father ten or fifteen minutes to get to her. But the girl next to her in line was friendly looking and a little bit fat. Mariska asked her if she ever watched *Strawberry Shortcake* and the girl said, "All the time!" and they began excitedly talking about that and the dream dissipated and Mariska woke up to credits rolling up the television screen and the room seemed too bright because no one had turned off the lights and she was freezing because the door was open and an icy wind had sucked all the fire's warmth from the room and the fire itself was only a bed of winking orange coals.

She stood up and walked over to the door.

"Dad?" she called out into the darkness. Sometimes, no matter how cold it was, he would go outside to smoke. Sometimes he smoked cigarettes that came in a red and white package and sometimes he rolled his own and sometimes he smoked a fat, smelly cigar.

When he didn't answer, she shut the door.

She locked it because that was what her mother told her she should always do when shutting the door to her house. Mariska walked through the kitchen and into the dining room. The light from her father's office was on and the door was open. She had never seen this door closed unless he wasn't in it, which he usually was. He didn't care about being bothered, but he didn't want anyone going through his stuff when he wasn't there. Mariska understood. She didn't like it when people played with her toys either.

His shoulders were slumped over the desk and he pecked slowly on his typewriter that she thought was the exact same color as her nipples.

"Sweetie?" he said without turning his head.

"I had a dream."

"Were you in your room?"

"No. On the floor."

"You shouldn't fall asleep on the floor."

She noticed a bottle of something the color of apple juice. This bottle looked fancier and was made from glass.

"Do you need me to tuck you in?" he said. He sounded ready to fall asleep himself.

"I'm thirsty." She now stood right beside him.

"Do you need me to get you some water?"

"What's that?" she pointed at the bottle.

He laughed a little. "That's bourbon, sweetie. It probably wouldn't make you less thirsty."

He offered her the bottle.

She brought it to her lips and recoiled at the smell. She handed it back.

She pointed at his nipple-colored typewriter and said, "Can I play on the typewriter?"

"Sure," he said. "This one's electric. See how it plugs into the wall? Do you want to play on this or the old typewriter?"

He pointed to one of the bookcases lining the walls. There was something that looked like the skeleton of what he currently pecked away at. She also thought it looked like it was made from coal.

She touched the electric typewriter and said, "This one."

"Okay. Maybe I need to stop vacuuming my brain for a minute anyway."

Her father never said he was writing. He was either "working" or "vacuuming his brain." He pushed back his chair, stood up, and stretched, the bones in his body making soft popping noises.

He put a couple of pillows in the chair, lifted her up, placed her down, and scooted the chair toward the desk.

"Remember," he said, "writing is the worst job in the world."

"I want a new one."

"Huh?"

"New paper."

"Oh. Of course. Collaboration is for the weak and simple minded."

He stripped out the piece of paper with his words on it and rolled a new one in.

"Have at it," he said.

She pecked out a few letters, hit the space bar, and pecked out the same letters because she liked them. He grabbed the key to one of his desk drawers from the top of the desk and dipped it into a little amber bottle. He quickly sniffed the key and put the bottle back into his pocket.

"Was that medicine?" She continued to peck at the keyboard, already feeling herself getting tired of it.

"Something like that." He grabbed the bottle of bourbon and sat down in the comfortable chair beside the desk. "Sometimes this makes me sleepy." He held the bottle up and took a slug. "And the other stuff wakes me up."

"If I had that medicine, I bet I wouldn't even *have* to take naps."

"And you probably wouldn't fall asleep in the middle of the floor."

She was now completely uninterested in the typewriter.

She turned to face him.

"Can we go look at the trees?" she asked.

"Why would you want to do that?"

She told him about her dream.

"We'll have to get you bundled up."

"Aren't you gonna read what I wrote?"

"Oh, of course. I wasn't sure if it was ready yet."

"It is. It's really good."

He leaned over the desk and read aloud. "Yog yog yog yog yog."

She started laughing. She didn't exactly know how to pronounce what she'd written and liked the way it sounded coming out of her father's mouth, like the sound a frog would make.

"That's really great. Very Lovecraftian." He placed a hand over the top of her head.

"Not the brain sucker!" she squealed.

He flexed his hand. "I think it's starving to death."

They crunched across the backyard. She wore her snow boots, her father's big wool coat, and one of his knit stocking caps.

"Aren't you cold?" she asked.

"I think the air feels nice."

The woods seemed a lot farther away in the winter than they did in the summer. When they reached the woods, he scooped her up and rested her on his hip.

"Is this okay or do we need to go into them?" he asked.

She studied the trees closely. There were maybe a few dead leaves clinging here and there to the ones that didn't have needles like a Christmas tree. But they were mostly bare.

"See," her dad said, "it was just a dream."

They turned and walked back to the house. The lights from the living room and her dad's office were still on, producing a warm glow. The back door was shut tight and, hopefully, not locked. She'd forgotten to tell him about the open door.

"Did you leave the door open earlier?" she asked.

"No. Why?"

"It was open when I woke up."

"Are you sure that wasn't just part of the dream?"

She looked back toward the woods. She couldn't see them at all now. They were just a gray mass in the distance. They hadn't been full of leaves. How could she be sure of anything?

"I don't know," she sighed.

When she looked toward the house, she focused on the

windows that didn't have light in them. She thought she saw shapes moving around in those dark rooms. Quick moving liquid shadows. They made her scared. Or maybe it was what her mom called anxious. Her mom had said that was like being scared when there wasn't really anything to be scared of.

"Will you read what I typed again?" she asked her father.

"Sure. When we get back inside. Okay?"

"I mean now. You remember, don't you?"

She thought it would make her laugh if she heard him say it again. It would make her less scared. Less anxious.

"*Yog*," he croaked.

She started laughing and wrapped her arms around his bony shoulders.

"*Yog yog yog*."

They stamped their feet and walked into the house where the fire was now completely dead.

He made her some hot chocolate and sipped bourbon. They watched *Strawberry Shortcake* until her head started to droop and then he picked her up and carried her into her bedroom.

"Are you going back to work?"

"Yeah, honey, I have to. Night night."

He gave her a peck on the forehead and disappeared into the yellow light of the hallway.

It was the last time she ever saw him.

Mariska had bypassed her car in town, deciding to take the ten-minute walk. She wasn't really much of an outdoors person. She felt like it would be better if she saw the house unencumbered by her car. She could linger. It was a good time for lingering. Probably not for much longer. The last few nights had been below freezing. Soon the town would be naked and cold, but she would be very far away from it. Although, she knew she'd probably be back.

The house was at the end of Spring Street, facing it, sitting low across a fairly large lawn. When her father lived there, when she used to visit him on the weekends, a series of three or four towering pine trees had stood behind the ugly guardrail. Those trees were gone now. They had been gone the last time too. The long gravel driveway was off a road farther down, so that the address was not actually Spring Street. She tried to remember what it was. Something Pike, maybe. She'd always used her mother's address as her own.

She stopped at the guardrail at the end of the road, almost close enough for her knees to touch its cold surface.

She stared at the house, at the couple windows that were lit up. Of course the light that came from windows was hardly ever a soft yellow anymore. Now it always seemed sterile – clear or bluish.

She never found out what happened to her father. She didn't think she wanted to find out. The thing that would have been best for him and probably the hardest for her to take was if he had just decided he'd had enough of his current life and left. If that were the case – and she really doubted it was – some part of her hoped he would make contact with her before he died. She had no clue what they would possibly say to one another. She didn't think she'd ever really known him very well and she was now very very far away from being daddy's little girl. But she had always felt close to him. Still did.

The door to the carport at the top of the driveway opened and her heart sped up like she'd been caught doing something she wasn't supposed to be doing.

A man walked out under the carport and lit a cigarette. He glanced at her but didn't make any gesture of acknowledgement. A woman who looked a little younger stepped out behind him and did the same. He said something to the woman that Mariska couldn't hear and they smiled and laughed. The woman playfully, almost seductively, punched him on the arm. They looked happy. Mariska knew she needed to go. She could already feel the house's power reaching for her. The memory of something frozen almost perfectly in time. The lure of contentment. The feeling of contentment would always be followed by the world crumbling beneath her feet.

THE EXISTENTIAL DREAD OF COMPLACENCY

1.

It was probably the first time in his adult life Thurston Tremont would readily admit to being happy with nearly everything. His teenage son was doing well, both physically and in school, and seemed to be less depressed than he had been a couple of years ago. Thurston only usually saw Matthew on the weekends and it didn't really feel like enough but, in reality, they probably spent more time together than many fathers and sons. After two failed marriages, Thurston was finally with a woman who had similar interests and complemented him. She felt as much like a friend as a lover and that was something he'd never really experienced before. He didn't like to think every relationship was supposed to make you miserable at least half the time. He didn't really know where that idea came from but figured it was probably some latent misogynist notion. The woman gave the man sex and therefore he must pay for that with his misery. It relegated all romantic relationships to prostitution, essentially. But this one didn't feel like that. Oh, and the sex was great. She was a writer, too, and they spent much of their time together sitting beside one another and working on their own projects in their individual heads. They came together to share. It worked. And the books were selling reasonably well. The past year or so had seen some newfound interest in the work of Holger Blackwell and the manuscript Thurston completed for his goonish editor, *The One Who Creeps*, earned him enough in royalties to pay his rent. And the rent wasn't as cheap as it had been this time last year. He and Kara had finally bitten the bullet and moved out of their scary, tiny, ancient, but cheap apartment in downtown Dayton to a house in the town of Twin Springs. She was from up north but had fallen in love with the town when he'd taken her there one weekend shortly after they'd first met. And he'd liked it ever since going there with his friends in high school. He and his friends had mainly gone there because of the head shop and bookstore and you could buy incense and anything else you needed to turn yourself into a goofy hippie overnight. But there was more to it than that. They went to high school in the middle of a cornfield in a conservative small town. It wasn't the small town he had a problem with. He loved small towns. He did not enjoy gun toting, racist, conservative small mindedness. Twin Springs was home to Shrine College. While it had fallen on hard times lately, there was a legacy of equality and progressive politics that was still palpable. Living somewhere where they were surrounded by dreadlocked, barefoot, patchouli wearing hippies was highly preferable to watching people get shot in the parking lot of the clubs across the street. Plus Holger Blackwell had lived there. Plus there were good restaurants to eat in and a brewery down the street that brewed awesome beer. And there were trees. A lot of trees. So they were somewhat shocked to find that the SWAT team had had to shoot the previous tenant out of the house for randomly firing his considerable arsenal out the window. They hadn't heard about the incident when it had happened. Living in

Dayton, they never followed the news. It was too depressing. Or horrifying. It seemed like things like that had happened every week. But they had Googled the address and it had come up. He and Kara liked things with a history so it definitely didn't want to make them back out of it. They'd almost *bought* a house in an area where they didn't really want to live just because it had a cemetery behind it and a tombstone in the backyard.

So he was perfectly willing to admit to himself that he was happy but the most he would ever be willing to admit to someone who asked was that he was doing "okay." Because every time he'd found himself complacent in his place in the world, it had ended up crumbling around him and then he was likely to spend the next two years picking up the pieces. It was entirely possible it was that history that would keep him from being a hundred percent content. Not that he thought anyone was ever really perfectly content. But he knew he could never rest. He always had to remain somewhat vigilant. Which was maybe why he liked to spend at least an hour every night staring into the darkness and thinking thoughts he would never write down or speak aloud. This, he thought, was how adults terrified themselves.

Or maybe he just liked the night and the quiet and the contemplative nature of that environment allowed his mind to open up and his mental guard to relax a little while he thought about all the bad things that could happen.

It made him want to drink and smoke more. By the third or fourth beer, the night air smelled great – full of honeysuckle and something almost spicy he couldn't identify – and Kara and he would be together forever, and they were in the perfect place and he couldn't ask for anything more from his writing career and, hey, even the day job wasn't that horrible.

He took a sip of beer and a deep breath before lighting another cigarette. Sometimes thinking was the worst thing a person could do. The only things easy to think about were appointments, how shitty your life was, or how you were going to go about conquering the world. Everything else was just so many shades of gray. The important thing was to find moments like this and squeeze every ounce of enjoyment from them and hope they would be abundant.

After all, when all was said and done, things were not that bad. And they could *always* be worse.

His and Kara's mutual friend, Dustin, was coming by the next day with his wife, Jessica. Thurston and Dustin shared the same deadbeat publisher. They'd wander around the town, eat good food, drink much beer, smoke many cigarettes, and trade gossip about their fellow degenerate writers.

It would be fun.

2.

Thurston got a text from Dustin saying they were almost there.

"Thank god. I'm starving." Kara put her hands over her tiny stomach like something inside of her was dying.

"I'm sure they'll be ready to get something to eat."

Thurston and Kara went out to the driveway just as the battered maroon minivan pulled in. They went around to the passenger side to greet Jessica as she got out of their van. It was both their opinion that the wives and girlfriends of their writer friends – mostly male – were woefully neglected if not completely ignored. Unless the wife was the publisher of the writer friend. This was the case with at least three of them. Thurston couldn't help noticing it looked like the back of the van was filled with trash. He wasn't really a judgmental person. It was just an observation.

Dustin had already crawled out of the driver's seat and come around to join them just as Jessica got out of the passenger side. Hellos made their rounds and they joined in a group hug. Jessica and Dustin smelled really bad. Thurston was pretty sure Jessica was pregnant. Something that had never come up.

"So you guys ready to go get some food?" he asked.

"Sounds great," Dustin said. "I hate to ask you this but is it okay if we take a quick shower first? I feel really ripe."

Of course people had asked to use the shower before, but this was the first time Thurston could recall anyone asking to use it upon arrival.

"Sure, man." Dustin and Jessica grabbed a couple of bags from the back of the van. Thurston led them into the house and Kara stayed behind to pick up the excess trash that had rolled from the van.

Dustin and Jessica dumped their bags inside the door off the carport and Thurston led them down the hallway to the bathroom. He grabbed a couple of towels and washcloths from the linen closet and held them out to Dustin.

"Here you go."

"Nah, man. We don't like the way any of that stuff feels on our skin."

Thurston stood somewhat frozen, continuing to hold out the towels and washcloths.

"So I should just . . . put them back?"

"Do whatever, man. We just need the water to get clean and the air to dry us off."

"Okay."

Thurston went to find Kara. Dustin and Jessica disappeared into the bathroom. Well, they didn't really *disappear* because neither one of them bothered shutting the door.

Kara sat at the small table on the bizarre back patio, smoking. A bag of Bugles sat on the table.

"I had to eat something," she said. "I was starving."

"Me too." Thurston sat down with a heavy groan.

He realized he probably didn't know Dustin and Jessica as well as he thought he did. Their publisher put together a convention in Seattle every year and the authors were encouraged to attend, even though the trip out there cost roughly three times what the publisher ever paid them in royalties. Kara and Thurston had found themselves hanging around the other couple quite a bit. But that wasn't really a normal environment and they weren't really in close quarters or anything. And, he guessed when he added it up over the course of a weekend "quite a bit" was probably closer to three hours. They'd also met Dustin at a reading in Chicago and spent a few hours drinking with him afterward. But that was just Dustin by himself, not with Jessica.

Thurston sighed. "It's going to be an interesting evening."

He told her about the towels.

"And who just shows up and asks to use the shower anyway?" Kara crushed out her cigarette and immediately lit another one. "I'm starting to wish we were already drunk when they got here."

Thurston pulled a cigarette from the pack and lit it. "Maybe it'll even out."

"I hope so. What time are they leaving tomorrow?"

"I don't know. I think they were headed on to Florida or someplace so I imagine they'd want to get on the road."

"Is Jessica pregnant?"

"I don't know. That's what I thought, too. Dustin hasn't mentioned it."

They smoked, stared into the thick woods, and listened to their stomachs grumble for nearly an hour.

"Not just any shower," Kara said. "The world's fucking longest shower."

"How bout all that weight they've lost though, huh?"

"I know, right? I was going to say they'd lost a lot of weight when they got out of the van but that's like saying, 'Hey, you were really fat!' I guess that's pretty much why we can't ask them if she's pregnant."

Thurston didn't really know if the weight loss was a good thing. The last time they'd seen the couple, they'd been probably a hundred pounds heavier. Some people lost weight through diet and exercise and they seemed to maintain some kind of healthful glow. Dustin and Jessica looked like they'd been starving themselves. They looked sick. He wondered if they'd lost their house or something. Maybe they had been living out of their van. Maybe that was the reason the inside of it looked the way it did. Maybe that's why they'd lost so much weight and smelled the way they did. He considered asking them about it. Maybe he would if he got Dustin alone later. But he almost didn't want to know the answer. If he knew the answer, he might feel compelled to help. He and Kara did okay financially, but he still had his son to support and the modest surplus they were left with was really only enough to eat out a couple of times a month – a luxury they'd come to enjoy and look forward to. That left offering them a place to stay. His son still used the one bedroom when he came over but there was the library. He supposed they could throw a futon or air mattress in there. But he was getting ahead of himself. He decided if they were too irritating, he just wouldn't ask.

The screen door opened and Dustin and Jessica came out.

They were both completely naked and dripping wet. They were covered in bruises and welts and Thurston couldn't help noticing that neither one of them did any bush work whatsoever.

Dustin pulled one of the wrought iron chairs out from the table and sat down heavily.

He wiped a hand across his wet brow and said, "Thanks, man. That felt great."

It was actually really hard to not like Dustin.

"No problem."

Thurston noticed Dustin and Jessica didn't really smell much better than when they had gone in. They probably hadn't used any soap, either.

"Just let us dry off for a little bit and we'll be ready to go. So what have you guys been up to?"

Jessica drifted off the patio and into the yard. She stared at the birds and tall trees and looked super stoned. Kids lived on the street and their yard was often used as a shortcut for people going into the woods so he considered calling her back but decided not to worry about it. She was an adult. She could get herself out of any situation she put herself into.

Kara and Thurston gave Dustin the rundown of the last few months. Kara provided the actual facts. Thurston provided the opinionated color.

Jessica wandered to the edge of the woods and stared into them. She may have been touching herself.

"So what's up with you guys?" Thurston asked.

Dustin was a talker, a great storyteller. It was one of the reasons he was so entertaining to have around. He just shrugged and said, "Not much."

Jessica came charging back to the patio and said, "I saw a rabbit!" before launching into a coughing fit.

The next few minutes of conversation were stilted and awkward.

Finally Thurston gave Dustin the once over and said, "You guys dry enough to put on some clothes and get something to eat?"

3.

Dustin and Jessica each wore some kind of dashiki-looking thing, only it looked like they were made out of some plain muslin-like material.

"You guys look like cult members or something," Kara said.

"Nah." Dustin chuckled, showing a shade of who he used

to be.

Their attire would have really embarrassed Thurston if they had been anywhere but Twin Springs. The place seemed to have a tolerance for that sort of thing whereas the rest of the Dayton area seemed to be almost aggressively normal.

They went to the all-organic, locally sourced Peruvian restaurant in town and had a great meal. Thurston and Kara rarely let their guests pay for anything and this was no exception. Besides, Thurston didn't see where Dustin or Jessica could possibly keep any means to pay. Their gown things were virtually transparent and didn't have any pockets. The conversation over dinner had been a little livelier although Dustin and Jessica seemed to be talking about things that had happened a really long time ago, like in their college days. There was still no clue about what they'd been up to in the last few months.

"Thanks for getting that," Dustin said as they left the restaurant. "We don't carry cash or credit cards anymore."

Kara and Jessica walked ahead of them, engaged in their own conversation.

"Are you serious?" Thurston thought maybe Dustin had been joking.

"Too confining."

"Then how do you pay for things?"

"We don't. Nobody should have to pay for anything."

"So . . . what? I should have just walked out on the check back there?"

"That would have been one option. Or we could just not have gone."

"So, okay, you don't buy food? I guess that explains how you guys have lost so much weight."

"Yeah. I feel great."

"But you have to eat."

"We do. Once we lost all that weight, we realized we don't really need that much to keep going."

"So you grow your own food or something?"

"A little. But that's a lot of work. We do take a few things off the shelf at the store but that's stuff they just throw out when it goes bad anyway."

"So you forage for the rest?"

"Yeah. Mostly. People throw away a lot of good shit."

"Oh, man. So you're dumpster diving?"

"Sure. Why not? It beats having to work to feed ourselves, you know?"

"But, dude, you're eating trash. Couldn't you work for a couple hours a day so you and your wife could eat something good every now and then?"

"We eat fine. Nobody used to really think about food. This obsession with food is just one indicator of the crumbling empire. Before the Roman Empire fell, people were eating until they vomited so they could eat more, adults introduced children into the world of sex, and a lot of other fucked up shit. Now we have the Food Network, reality television, and Facebook. Oh, and rich white men going on sex tours through Asian and Eastern European countries so they can fuck kids. Think about it."

The conversation had taken a grim turn. Thurston wanted to get back to the house so they could start drinking soon. Hopefully, Dustin and Jessica still drank. Hopefully it wasn't too emblematic of the crumbling empire. Wait, he thought. They still didn't know if Jessica was pregnant or not. She probably wouldn't drink if she was pregnant. He'd asked Dustin about the weight loss and regretted it. If anyone was going to ask Jessica about being pregnant, it would have to be Kara. He and Kara had had four growlers filled at the brewery earlier so either Dustin and Jessica were going to help drink it or Thurston and Kara were going to go into a coma. And if Jessica happened to be out, well, that just meant more for the rest of them. The way things were going, he was pretty sure he was going to need it.

"Besides," Dustin continued, "it's not just about working a couple hours a day so you can eat. It's about conforming to a whole system. You can't just take bits and pieces of capitalism. You have to eat the whole thing. And then you're locked into the game because if you don't compete you feel like a loser. It teaches you to want more and more things, better and better things, but it keeps the ultimate goal forever out of reach. Sure, people will work increasingly difficult jobs or increasingly long hours to try and get that shit but the only people who ever do get it are the people who were pretty much born into it in the first place. And they don't even appreciate it! They have to spend money on ways to fill their copious amount of free time, which is probably the only thing someone like you wants more of."

Thurston had fazed out a bit. "Huh?"

"Free time. That's what you would say you work hard for, right? You guys barely own anything."

"Sure. I guess."

"Well, see, I have plenty of that and I don't work at all. All I'm saying is: would you rather work eight hours and eat something you bought from someplace that, let's face it, still isn't that great, or would you rather have eight hours of free time and choke down an old burger you found in a McDonald's trashcan?"

"It's a little more than that. I don't want the thought of where my next meal is coming from to occupy my entire brain. Plus I have insurance and child support payments to make."

"Yeah, but what if your day job goes under and people stop buying your books?"

"I try not to think about any of that."

"I'm just saying we're probably ten years away from being a third world country. We've let the rich siphon off all the excess that was supposed to be distributed amongst the people and it's thrown things out of balance. There's no way this country can sustain itself."

They were approaching the house.

"Man, I could really use a drink. You guys still drink, don't you?" Maybe now he would find out if Jessica was pregnant or not.

"Fuck yeah," Dustin said. "As long as we don't have to pay for it."

Thurston wasn't sure if he was joking or not.

4.

It took about midway through the second growler before Dustin knocked off the adolescent political rhetoric and started to relax a little. Thurston actually agreed with most of what he said but found it overly idealistic and a horribly boring topic for party conversation. He'd always felt more than three people constituted a party and while Jessica was technically a fourth person the beer had taken what little contribution she had made out of her. She seemed almost zombified. Thurston relaxed a little. If she drank she probably wasn't pregnant. Maybe the rounded belly had something to do with malnourishment, like those starving African kids they showed on tv.

The conversation shifted to writing and publishing, as it usually did with them. Jessica lost the last shred of interest she had in the conversation, shed her clothes, and wandered out in the yard to dance. It was dark and the light didn't reach that far and Thurston was glad because it would have made him nervous to look at her. When they began talking about some of their writer friends and the people they knew in publishing, Thurston was alarmed by the vitriolic hatred that came from Dustin. He used to be the type of person to find people's quirks funny. There were plenty of negative things to be said – it wasn't a perfect world – but everyone was pretty much there by choice and doing something they presumably enjoyed doing so Dustin's complete eviscerations of people seemed a bit much. Kara, already pretty drunk, laughed at much of what Dustin said but Thurston thought, with the way he was saying it, it wasn't really a laughing matter.

A dog howled in the distance. A June bug dive bombed the candle in the middle of the patio table and jerked convulsively in the wax, giving everyone a start. Jessica was nowhere to be seen, although Thurston was pretty sure he could hear her moving and panting.

Kara scrolled through her phone and read some Facebook posts from people they knew. Most of them were idiotic. Thurston was pretty sure the act of saying you did something cool on Facebook completely sucked the cool from it.

When they exhausted that, Thurston asked Dustin what he was working on.

"Nothing, man."

"Nothing?"

"What's the point?"

"I thought you liked doing it."

"Nah. It was stupid and childish. I said everything I had to say. I guess I'll write another one if I feel like I have something else to say."

Thurston liked Dustin's writing a lot, but he'd never thought of it as being particularly philosophical.

"The publishing business is just modern day slavery, anyway. You have a hundred slaves working for pennies so the publishers can get rich by, what? Uploading a couple of files?"

Thurston thought comparing a group of what was mostly middle age, middle-to-upper-middle class white guys to slavery was nearly offensive but, that aside, Thurston couldn't really disagree with him. It was one of the reasons he and Kara self-published most of their stuff these days. He was still pretty sure no one in the small press world was getting rich.

Kara tapped out sometime during the third growler. Jessica still had not joined them. The woods were alive with insect sounds. Heat lightning strobed the sky.

Kara told Dustin where the extra blankets and pillows were.

"Thanks but we'll probably just sleep out here."

Her hospitality thwarted, Kara disappeared into the house without saying anything else.

"You don't have to sleep outside."

"No. I know, man. Thanks for the offer. We just like it better outside. Indoors is too confining. Jessica's really sensitive to mold and mildew. She says she can smell it every time she's inside."

"There's probably more mold and mildew outside than in."

"I know, but it belongs there."

This seemed somewhat irrational to Thurston but he let it drop.

He was finally drunk enough to let his curiosity force him to ask what had happened.

"So what the hell happened, man? What have you guys been doing since we saw you the last time?"

"What do you mean?"

"Come on. I'm not the only one who's asked you about this, am I? Didn't you move out here to be closer to your parents? What do they think?" Thurston almost hoped this was where Dustin would come clean and tell him they'd moved back in with his parents. That would have made some things make a little more sense.

"We don't speak to my parents anymore."

"I thought you were close."

"They're government workers. I wouldn't feel comfortable

talking to them until they quit their jobs."

"But they're both teachers. Most people see teachers as saints."

"Well we see them as tools in the government brainwashing conspiracy."

"Are you fucking serious?"

"Of course I'm serious."

Thurston wanted to ask him to go back to being the old Dustin, a fun person to be around. Crazy, perhaps, but crazy in a good way.

"So that's what you've been doing? Working on some kind of . . . manifesto that will gradually eliminate everyone you know from your life?"

"It's not really like that. Once you reaffirm your personal beliefs it just makes hypocrisy impossible."

"So would continuing to talk to your parents be hypocrisy?"

"Are you kidding? I know what it is they stand for. I know where their money comes from. And I know they're unwilling to change."

"So just spending time with them because they're your parents and forgetting about all the other stuff is hypocritical?"

"Yes."

"I guess I just don't understand the rigidity of your thinking."

"That's because you want a comfortable life so you keep your morals and personal philosophy liquid and amorphous."

"Is that a bad thing?"

"It's not for me."

"So how can you talk to me knowing that I pay taxes, thus supporting the system you hate so much?"

"Because you have to do that. You have a job."

Thurston lit a cigarette and took a big gulp of beer. "We need to stop talking about this shit. Did Jessica ever come back?"

"I'm right here." She stood less than a foot behind Thurston and he jumped when she spoke.

"Jesus fucking Christ," he said, immediately standing up. "And with that, I think I'm going to call it a night. Help yourself to what's left of the beer. I'll leave the door unlocked. There's a bed inside if you decide you don't want to sleep in the yard."

5.

Thurston lay in bed and stared at the ceiling. If he were as drunk as he'd hoped to be, he would have passed right out. But the last few minutes of talking with Dustin had made him almost inexplicably angry and Jessica finally sneaking up on him had scared him completely sober. Now he was just mostly tired and wanted to go to sleep.

That was hard because Jessica and Dustin were still on the patio and that wasn't very far from his open bedroom window. It sounded like they were arguing. He wondered what Jessica could have been doing in her time away from them. There was no way she'd been dancing around in the yard for something close to three hours. And all that shit Dustin was talking about? He almost hoped it was some kind of elaborate put on.

He heard them move around to the front of the house, their voices escalating into near hysterical violence.

Kara was still dead to the world.

Thurston decided to get up and see what was wrong before someone down the street called the cops.

A dim light glowed from the van.

The screaming and yelling continued from the inside.

Thurston wasn't exactly sure how you approached people living in a van. He knocked on the window of the sliding door, realizing again how old the van was.

The door slid back and Dustin said excitedly, "She's crowning!"

"Huh?"

Thurston felt dazed. He thought, somewhere deep inside his memory, he should know what that meant.

"Jessica's having the baby."

"Shouldn't . . . we call someone?"

Dustin hopped out of the van and wrapped his hands around Thurston's arms.

"You don't understand. This is the sacrifice we've been waiting for. Once the child is born we must take it to the place in the woods where Jessica's water broke and bathe in its blood. I have the ceremonial knife right here." Dustin held it up as proof. "If we do this, no one in attendance will ever have to do anything they don't want. Do what thou wilt!"

"I don't think I can let you do that." Thurston was already sliding his phone out of his pocket. It was dead. He wasn't completely surprised. It seemed like there were a hundred apps he couldn't figure out how to keep from running.

Kara stumbled out of the house just as the first volley of

the baby's cries came from the van.

"I need the knife to cut this fucking cord!" Jessica shouted.

A dog howled in the distance. Insects hummed around him. A shadow or possibly the clouds moved across the moon.

"What the fuck is going on?" Kara still looked half-asleep.

"Do you have your phone on you?"

"No. It's in the house. Why?"

How to tell her . . . Thurston wondered if he should bother explaining or just start shouting for help.

"Thurse, what the fuck is going on?"

"We need to call the cops or an ambulance or something. Jessica just delivered her baby. They want to take it into the woods and sacrifice it."

"Okay."

"*Okay?*"

"It's not our place to stop them."

This journalistic approach was expected with most things, but he didn't see how this didn't get more of a reaction from her.

"I can't let them go through with this. Kill a baby?"

She shrugged. "Are we allowed to watch?"

Jessica must have drugged and brainwashed Kara. That was the only excuse Thurston could think of. Maybe Jessica had sneaked into her room after she'd gone to bed. Maybe she'd slipped her something at dinner and had been working on her subliminally ever since.

Dustin and Jessica came around from the back of the van, Dustin holding the baby swaddled in Jessica's robe. Dustin beamed. Jessica looked weak, her thighs splashed with blood.

What if there is *no baby?* Thurston wondered.

Since he was the only one not going along with this, he thought maybe they were all playing a trick on him. Deep down, he knew that couldn't be the case. He found himself following them around to the back of the house. Jessica had definitely given birth. He'd seen her naked earlier and there was no way she hadn't been pregnant. And now she was definitely not pregnant. When he'd seen her come around from the back of the van the firm baby bump had been replaced with what looked like two feet of stretch marked, saggy skin. And this was the first time they'd all been together in nearly a year. Why would the three of them want to spend all night acting just for some kind of ridiculous payoff?

Thurston thought he would almost rather believe anything than what was actually happening around him.

"Dustin, man, I can't let you do this." He felt like he had to say something, but felt powerless to stop it.

Dustin was suddenly in front of him, brandishing the knife with the hand that wasn't holding the sacrificial infant in a bloody robe.

"We're going through with this!" There was a look in his eyes Thurston had never seen before. "You can get the fuck away, but you're not stopping us. If you try to stop us, I'll cut your fucking throat."

Thurston thought about how this would look on a police report, maybe even in front of a jury, and wondered if it would let him off the hook as an accomplice. He put up his hands in a gesture of defeat.

Kara placed a hand on Thurston's arm. "Just calm down."

"Yeah," Jessica smiled. "That's *my* pussy fruit."

The moon was nearly if not completely full and the backyard was fairly well lit. Maybe someone would see them and do something. But who would see? The strange man Kara sometimes swore she saw lurking around the house? He really felt like he should turn and run for help. There were probably only a few minutes left.

As they stepped into the dark wood, he felt the last vestiges of protest leave his body. He felt like he was on acid or some other, more euphoric drug. The woods were dark but seemed to almost glow and pulse. He imagined an umbilical cord running from the woods to the house and briefly wondered which way the nutrients were going. Which was feeding which. Jessica and Dustin and Kara all seemed to be panting as they headed deeper into the woods and Thurston heard the dog howl again. This time it was almost deafeningly close and he saw that the dog, a huge black thing, was right in front of them. It lowered its head from the unobservable moon and began lapping at the ground. Thurston thought that must be where Jessica's water broke. And now Jessica stood in front of the dog and the dog began licking the afterbirth from her thighs and in between her legs. She lay on her back and spread her legs. The beast's member was huge and pink and dripping as it moved on top of her and began thrusting. Dustin slashed at the swaddle he held in his left arm. His eyes were huge and he smiled crazily. He held the baby aloft above the dog fucking his wife, the blood raining down and coating all of them.

"Do what thou wilt shall be the whole of the law!" he shouted over and over, dancing around the scene of bestiality being played out on the floor of the woods.

Thurston felt assaulted by the night and the woods. He felt

the moon and the leaves and the dirt and every droplet of water on his skin. He smelled blood and sex and dog and something spicy and exotic and not entirely unpleasant. Everything spun and throbbed around him and the last thing he remembered was collapsing onto his hands and knees and vomiting onto the ground, Kara's cool hand on the back of his neck.

6.

He woke up very late the next afternoon.

His body felt stiff and abused but, thankfully, there was no trace of the nausea he'd felt last night.

Kara had already made coffee. Recently, it smelled like. She probably hadn't gotten out of bed long before him.

Last night came back to him in vivid, nightmarish detail.

He poured a cup of coffee and looked out at the driveway. There was no sign of Dustin and Jessica's hideous van.

He took his coffee out to the back patio and sat down next to Kara. He reached for the cigarettes and lit one.

He wondered if they would talk about it.

He didn't really want to.

Talking about it seemed like it would make it real.

But it was real.

He denied that thought. He felt like it was something that needed the shape of words to make it more complete.

"Sleep well?" Kara looked toward the dark woods.

"Like a baby," he said.

KING CREEP

1.

He found it best if he thought of himself as his stage persona – Slade Kontrol. Only there wasn't really a stage. Just a couch in the middle of his mostly bare living room, a girl who was barely of legal age (he had a photocopy of her driver's license and social security card) sitting in the middle of the couch, one huge black guy to her left massaging himself through his tight jeans, a large white guy to her right massaging himself through his basketball shorts, and himself, standing behind a camera on a tripod. Currently the only thing in the frame of the camera was the girl – Sierra Leone. He wondered if she knew where Sierra Leone was. He wondered if she even knew it was a country. Young, natural, pretty, wearing a pair of black yoga pants and a sleeveless t-shirt. She didn't look like a porn star. Really, at his level, there were no porn stars. This amounted to, essentially, filmed prostitution. Some girls he'd filmed had taken the leap out to California and made something of a name for themselves, but most of them were lazy and poor or they wouldn't need the money in the first place and most of them had a laundry list of things they wouldn't do, although that often relaxed depending on how high or drunk they were. This one had specifically said no anal, no choking, and they could come anywhere but inside of her. In Slade's experience, this usually meant they had a boyfriend who would want to fuck them later and didn't know how they made their money. It was an interesting moral code. The girl had no problems with him and his two actors fucking her senseless for an hour or so but the thought of her boyfriend fucking through another man's come would just be too humiliating for him.

"What's your name?" he started the only thing close to a script. He had it dedicated to memory, pretty much.

"Sierra Leone." She smiled but still looked nervous.

"How old are you, Sierra?"

"I just turned eighteen."

"Great. Now you can buy cigarettes, pornography, and join the army. How many guys have you had sex with?"

She held up two fingers.

"How old were you when you had sex for the first time?"

"Thirteen."

"How old was your boyfriend?"

"Well, he wasn't my boyfriend. Just some guy. He was probably sixteen or seventeen."

"Do you have a boyfriend now?"

She nodded slowly.

"Does he know you're doing this?"

She shook her head.

"Do you think you'll fuck him later?"

"I'm going to tell him I don't feel like it, but he'll probably want to anyway."

"So why are you here?"

She'd been told not to say anything about money or drugs. Some of them did, but he just edited that out.

"It seemed like fun."

"Have you ever had more than one guy at a time before?"

She shook her head. "I've always wanted to but doing it with guys I knew seemed strange, you know? Like I'm pretty sure it would change things or they'd talk about me or something, you know?"

"Some people might see this."

She shrugged.

He told most of the girls he didn't advertise in their home state and a surprising amount of them believed him. Like he could even really control that. He felt like they probably knew what the internet was and were just in some kind of denial. In actuality, phase one of the advertising campaign (besides uploading a two minute clip to every free service on the web) was to send emails to accounts registered in the closest proximities to this zip code with: OMG! DO YOU KNOW THIS GIRL! in the subject line and a very clear picture of the actress' face in the body with a link to the two minute clip.

Slade continued to walk through the script. He didn't feel bad about what he did. It was legal, these girls were adults, and he never forced them to make this decision. He placed an ad as a modeling agency, they responded via email with some usually very deceptive photos attached. He wasn't that into fat girls so he just never responded to those emails. If he responded it was to make an appointment for them to come to the house. He didn't live here. He lived in a much nicer house in town. If they showed up and they were too fat or ugly to film, he asked them a few questions about their modeling experience and told them they weren't what he was looking for or, if they seemed especially delicate, that they just didn't have enough experience. If they were someone he wanted to film, he explained to them what they would be doing and, if possible, began filming within the next few minutes. A lot of girls said they needed time to think about it and left even after he offered to pay them a lot more and tried his best coercion tactics. A few of those girls got back with him but most did not. If they were up to it, they had either come in expecting what they were "auditioning" for or were up for just about anything all the time. Usually because they needed money. Probably because they had a drug habit. They were the party girls. He wasn't really sure about Sierra. Probably just bored.

"Okay, Sierra, stand up and let's get a good look at you."

She stood up. The camera ran up and down her body.

"Turn around."

She turned around. The camera focused on her ass.

"Okay. Now do you mind getting down on your knees and sucking my cock?"

She stared into the camera before looking away.

Someone was knocking on the door. It was typically Slade's policy not to answer it. He was always afraid of opening the door to find some murderously jealous redneck boy-friend standing there with a shotgun.

This girl paid more attention to it than most. Maybe *she* was afraid it was her boyfriend.

Slade rarely shut the camera off. There had been a couple of girls who'd freaked out during filming. One had com-plained that the guy was too big and had started, literally, cry-ing "Rape!" Slade turned off the camera, calmed her down, let her smoke some heroin, and finished the scene with about a half a tube of lube. Thank god that shit was a write off. The other girl he'd suspected was crazy and kept yelling lies about how he'd gotten her here. But, with the rise of YouTube and some non-pornographic clips going viral in a mainstream sort of way and gaining sponsorship, Slade always thought it best to keep the camera running. As long as there wasn't anything legally damning to him.

"Do you know who that might be?"

She shook her head.

"Are you sure you didn't tell your boyfriend you were here?"

"No. Why would I do that? Everyone knows what you do in this house."

This was, actually, somewhat of a shock to Slade. He supposed it was inevitable that people in a small town would talk, but he assumed the nature of what he did would be too embarrassing for anyone to substantiate with firsthand knowledge.

"Do you want to answer the door, Sierra?"

"Were you just going to let them keep knocking?"

"Well . . . yeah."

"I can get it, I guess."

"Dude, I gotta split in, like, an hour," Black Brian said.

That was actually his two actors' "thing". Most of the time they were billed as "The Brothers Brian." They clearly were not brothers. They were, respectively, Black Brian and White Brian. They even had matching tattoos – the yin and yang symbol except, yes, with a black penis and a white penis. The adult film industry was not known for political correctness.

"I'm sure it's nothing," Slade said.

Sierra was already headed for the door off the carport. It was not, technically, the front door but since it was the one that usually had the outside light on beside it, it was the one people usually came to.

"You care if we step out and smoke?" White Brian asked.

"Just a cigarette?" Slade said.

"Yeah, man."

"Whatever."

Slade found that when some guys smoked pot it made them soft and he usually had to edit out fifteen minutes of them viciously jerking off before launching the money shot. The Brothers Brian were both so huge it looked like they rarely achieved full erections anyway. Slade didn't want to play with fire.

The Brians went out to the wonky back patio through the door in the living room.

The door to the carport was mostly glass so there wasn't any need for a peephole.

Before Sierra could open the door, Slade said, "Wait a minute."

This guy looked weird. He was bald but a lot of guys were. Maybe the harsh fluorescent from the porch light made him look paler than he actually was. But it wasn't just the washed out, almost bleached pallor of his skin. He had no eyebrows. And Slade thought that if he were to be standing closer to him, he probably wouldn't find any eyelashes either.

He stood there, dressed like a middle-age dad or a guy on vacation, staring blankly at the door. He methodically raised his right hand and knocked.

"Can I help you?" Slade called through the door.

The man quit knocking and stared intently at the door. Slade wasn't sure how well he could see inside. Slade checked the camera and made sure everything was still focused and in frame.

"I need . . . help. There's been an accident."

"Have you called someone?" Slade asked. He was getting some kind of weird, bad vibe coming off this guy.

The man continued to stand in that odd way and stare at the door. Slade looked through the camera and zoomed it forward a little to see if he could maybe get a better look at this guy without actually opening the door. The man stared straight into the camera.

"Please. I need . . . help. There's been an accident."

"Go ahead and open the door," he told Sierra.

It took him only a couple of seconds to process the reasons for doing this. First, there was always a need to catch something interesting on camera. Now that he had the chance to do that, he wasn't going to send the guy away because he didn't want to deal with him. And the man didn't look dangerous. He wasn't holding a gun or any other type of weapon. He was fairly slight of build and seemed genuinely dazed. Also, this guy was only one man while Slade was surrounded by three people, two of which were about the size of small cars.

The man stumbled past them, into the kitchen, on his way to the living room, almost like he knew where he was going.

"I just . . . I really need to sit down."

The man headed for the couch.

"Call 911," Slade said to Sierra.

She walked over to the couch, Slade focusing the camera on her ass as she reached down and fished her phone from her purse. He noticed she wore black underwear. He was already lamenting the fact that he might not get to see her out of those underwear.

There was a bright flash from outside. Like *really* bright.

It didn't help that the wall facing the backyard was almost all glass. There was a second where everything in the room was almost like an x-ray. He put the camera down and tried to blink away the black spots.

"What the fuck was that?" Sierra said.

"I don't know."

The man on the couch stared forward and blinked.

"You guys see that?" Slade called to the Brians through the screen door.

"Fuck yeah, man!" Black Brian called.

"You hear anything?" Slade asked.

"Nah, dude. Just that light."

Sierra scowled down at her phone.

"The battery's dead," she said.

Slade was momentarily excited. He thought maybe they had just witnessed something special and wondered if he'd managed to capture it on his camera. But his hopes sank before he could even focus on the viewfinder. The camera was dead.

"Fuck," he mumbled.

He sat the camera on the tv stand behind him and pulled out his phone.

It was dead too.

"Hey!" he called through the screen door. "Either of your phones work!"

"Nah, man!" Black Brian said.

"Fuck!" White Brian called. Slade assumed that meant his wasn't working either.

"Shit," he said.

Sierra stood there looking nervous.

"I don't think I wanna do this anymore," she said.

"We need to get help, I think," Slade said. "Can you go knock on a neighbor's door or drive to the police station or something?"

"I think I just want to go home."

She bent to grab her bag and began walking to the front door. Slade didn't really want her to leave but he didn't really know what to say and he was too distracted by the guy on the couch to think of anything. He guessed he could tell her not to bother contacting him the next time she needed money but, for what he was paying her and for what she would be doing, that didn't really make a lot of sense. He found himself staring at her very nice ass as she walked into the dining room, saying nothing. She left in that silent way and it seemed to plunge the house into a vacuum.

The Brothers Brian were still outside.

How long had it been since they'd opened the door for this man?

Probably only a couple of minutes but it felt much longer.

"I . . . I really need help," the man said.

He wasn't bleeding and it didn't look like there was anything outwardly wrong with him. Slade wondered if he'd been sent here strictly to fuck up his night.

"Hold on," he said. "We'll get you some help."

Just when he thought about running to the neighbor's house – a fairly good jaunt – it occurred to him that he could try plugging his phone in. He didn't know what would suck the life from every battery in the house, but it might have affected the neighbors too. He went into the bedroom and grabbed the charging cable for his phone. If this didn't work, it would probably be easier to get in the car and drive to the police station. That would only take around five minutes. Whatever was wrong with this guy, he didn't want him dying in the house.

2.

Alopecia universalis was the diagnosis Dr. Benway had given Alexander Lords' mother. Complete loss of body hair. It had happened overnight. He was twelve at the time. Now while most boys were talking wonderingly about their burgeoning pubic hair, Alexander was left to inspect himself from head to toe, hoping it would come back. It felt like some kind of outward stigma to what had happened that night, not that he felt it was anything to be ashamed of. So maybe stigma wasn't the right word. Maybe it was more of a trade off.

He wouldn't have kept it a secret if his mother hadn't told him to.

He'd finished watching *Blossom* and gone to bed. To him, and especially in retrospect, it seemed like one of the strangest shows on television. Something that had to be some kind of vehicle for a particularly nepotistic Hollywood family. He appreciated the character of Blossom. She was ugly by Hollywood standards, he guessed, but it was never really mentioned. Anything else and she would have been cast specifically as the ugly friend. Her friend on the show, Six, Alexander found oddly alluring. When he thought about her in later years, he remembered her as almost a midget and wasn't really sure why. Despite his curiosity, he could never bring himself to go back and watch it. It was probably her forehead, which had become enormous in his memory. There was Blossom's brother, Joey Lawrence. Alexander couldn't recall what his name had been on the show. He thought it was Joey but that didn't seem right. He wore a lot of clothes and was really cool. He had a lot of floppy, feathered hair that Alexander aspired to. This would later leave him feeling much animosity. Enough to where he'd apparently blocked out almost every scene Joey Lawrence was in. The most intriguing character for Alexander was the father of the family, played by Ted Wass. The supposed premise of the show was a bedraggled middle-aged dad was forced to raise his tough guy loose cannon son and ugly daughter by himself, while his daughter's big headed midget friend came to hang out. Alexander couldn't remember if the mother had run off or died. He was pretty sure she had died. The intriguing thing to Alexander was that Ted Wass seemed supremely miscast as a tv dad. He looked sinister, evil. Like he should be playing a crime boss in a daytime soap opera. Or even a thug in a horror or crime movie. Almost anything except a single dad. But maybe it was the Cosby effect. The theory that you could soften anyone by throwing a sweater on him. This inevitably led Alexander to think that Ted Wass was *not* a good father and the real story, *Blossom*'s real narrative, was what happened when the camera wasn't running. This was what Alexander thought about as he lay in bed the night he was abducted by aliens and lost all his hair.

It was exactly as dramatic as the few abduction stories he'd heard up to that point and all the ones he would hear afterward. This was at least a couple of years before *The X Files*, but he would later watch that show with the intensity most adolescent boys reserved for sports and pornography.

He lay in bed thinking of Ted Wass as an abusive father and suddenly his room was filled with a white-bluish light. His mother rented the house from an old college friend and loved the town. The only thing Alexander really liked was the bookstore. He was more of an indoor kid.

He felt the odd sensation of leaving his body. He'd had a spinal tap once and there had been a queasy type of pressure that had felt almost like it came from *inside* his body. This was a lot like that, except it was all over rather than concentrated in one area of his lower back. He tried to scream but it felt muffled or . . . or like he lacked the physical ability to scream. Like that ability was left with his physical body that he was sucked out of and raced increasingly far from. He was a relatively anxious, panicky kid, but found that as he drew farther from his body a great sense of peace and calm began to envelop him. Where he went was mostly indescribable. He was aware of shapes around him and, maybe, they were roughly what the general descriptions of aliens were. But there was no real concrete sense of place. He couldn't remember any rooms or buildings or trees or landmarks or structures of any kind. It was like visiting a feeling. There were some colors he could recall – pinks and blues and glowing soft whites – but they were all fuzzy and throbbing, gaining and lessening in intensity almost like those cheap fiber optic things that had once been all the rage. It was like being surrounded by calm and peacefulness and tranquility with a deep eroticism humming just below the surface. This was the first time Alexander had felt this particular sensation. Of course he was as aware of his penis as most adolescent boys but he had not yet masturbated and was not aware of the feelings his sexual organs could produce. So this was all new. His penis was so hard it was nearly painful. It was like every surface of his skin was being touched sensuously at the same time. He was even aware of something moving into his anus, which he knew he wasn't supposed to like but kind of did. Of course all of this was an abstraction. He knew his eyes were open because he could see the shapes and colors but when he tried to train them on his body he was only aware that there was something that lacked specificity in its place. This was what he would later think of as his spirit body. After being there for what couldn't have been more than a few minutes, he didn't want to be anywhere else. And it continued for what felt like a very long time. That feeling in his groin would reach some pinnacle of pleasure – what he later learned was called an orgasm – and remain at that heightened level the entire time.

There wasn't an abrupt departure. He gradually became aware of leaving that place. It was like his spirit body, his alien body, had been almost large enough to encompass the whole earth and gradually shrunk into the little boy lying in his bed in Twin Springs.

He stared at his ceiling.

It felt like the life had been sucked out of the room.

He expected his mother to come rushing in or for there to be a whole fleet of emergency vehicles waiting for him. How long had he been away? It felt like he'd aged years or like he'd gained years of experience.

He looked at his clock. It was a wind-up alarm clock that read 10:04.

Later it would occur to him that, were it digital, it would have probably just flashed 12:00 at him and if it had run off a battery it probably would have been completely dead.

When he woke up the next morning, all of his body hair was gone. His mother was the first to discover this and began screaming hysterically. Alexander told her about the aliens and the only time she almost believed him was as she marveled over the absence of shed hairs in his bed.

The loss of hair bothered Alexander but, even at that young age, he understood a sacrifice had to be made.

He didn't go to school that day.

His mother had made an appointment with Dr. Benway who'd asked him a lot of questions and provided not a lot of answers. His mother was with him the entire time. He told Dr. Benway about the aliens. His mother asked the doctor if he thought Alexander had been molested. Benway said he could examine Alexander for that too, and made Alexander spread his butt cheeks so he could peer at his anus. Alexander said nobody had touched him in that way because he'd already told them about the aliens. He hadn't told them the way it made his penis feel because he thought that was private. Benway told Alexander that if he kept talking about aliens, he could make an appointment with a child psychiatrist. The only person Alexander knew who saw a child psychiatrist was Chad Hanger and he chewed on girls' hair and occasionally shit himself in class. Alexander decided to stop talking about aliens, but that didn't stop him from reading and watching everything about them he could get his hands on. His mother probably saw this as further proof he'd made the whole thing up, even though he had not been remotely interested in aliens before the abduction.

The aliens did not contact him again until he was twenty-four, a fairly recent graduate of Ohio State University, and working as a data entry specialist at a major health insurance company in Dayton.

He had to find a child and take it to the woods behind that old house his mom had rented for probably only a year back in the nineties. Of course Alexander knew exactly where the house was. That was where *it* had happened in the first place. Ever since getting his driver's license, he'd driven by it several times. He knew it was the aliens telling him to do this because it was an *alien* thought. One he'd never had before. He knew he was attracted to young boys sexually, although this was something he'd never acted on. He had simply resolved not to put himself around them. Oh, there was a time when he'd considered entering the priesthood to gain unlimited access but, in the end, he knew it was wrong, could see it being a potential problem, and resolved to stay away. He even had every intention of becoming a middle school science teacher when he started college. He had convinced himself he just wanted to teach kids about the stars but, before so much as even shadowing a teacher in a local middle school, he had become aware of the real reason and promptly switched his major to a degree in general science. That was something he was genuinely interested in. He found himself working where he did because he needed a job and they were looking for someone with a degree, any degree, it didn't matter.

The alien thoughts did not announce themselves as perfectly formed things. He did not hear a loud voice in his head saying: ALEXANDER, YOU NEED TO ABDUCT A

CHILD. No. It was a revelation he usually stumbled upon after some kind of intuition. Once he did stumble upon it – and this had, thus far, been the most potentially life altering one – they were impossible to shake. The communications became immediate obsessions. When he received this particular one, he remembered exactly what he was doing. He sat at his desk in the huge open office on the second floor, gazing toward Angela Bent's desk. It was a Friday afternoon, not long before they'd be walking out for the weekend. Three of their coworkers were gathered around her desk. Alexander got it. Angela was what these guys found attractive. Therefore, he should have probably found her attractive, as well. But he didn't. He'd never met a man or a woman he had been attracted to. Well, not since he'd been about twelve. That he was still attracted to people that age – particularly boys but a few tomboyish girls as well – didn't strike him as particularly mysterious. Psychologically, he'd never really gone through the full rite of puberty. He'd never graduated to the next level, so to speak.

He went back to entering data from the sheets before him when that intuition became crystal clear.

Really? I need to find a child and take it to the woods behind 523 Glowers Pike?

Yes. That was what he needed to do. He would have to figure out the specifics. He would have to figure out if this was even in his moral universe. There was no real timeline. No rush. The aliens' sense of time was not like his.

Nevertheless, he found himself eager to get started.

He left work and sat around his tiny apartment that weekend mostly figuring out ways to abduct his first child. He couldn't write anything down. He realized there would be *very serious* consequences if he was ever caught and the worst thing in the world would be to create any sort of paper or data trail. This was much the same reason he'd never so much as viewed what was popularly called child pornography. The closest he'd come were some art books he'd found in a bookstore two cities away. There was no way he would buy them or even steal them. He had taken them into the restroom, even though a posted sign had expressly forbid it. In a stall he had perused the books and, yes, shamefully, he'd ended up masturbating. It did not take long. It never did. Even when the only thing he had was mental porn conjured from his memories of the couple times he'd had to shower with the boys at gym class and the one summer he'd gone to camp.

The first and most obvious question was where he was going to get this child. The farther away the better. But it couldn't be so far away that he couldn't return home to his apartment. He wouldn't want his neighbors to notice his absence.

He would probably need to cull them from lower middle class or lower class neighborhoods. This wouldn't be a problem. Those types of people tended to breed more than the others and their parents were often more inattentive and the areas underpoliced. He would want to be as far away from the scene of the abduction as possible before anyone even noticed the child's absence.

His was pretty much a blank slate. His body type was average in every way. As long as he properly disguised himself he didn't think being seen was a big problem.

He decided he would have to try to fit in at work more, so he didn't fit the spot on profile of a serial killer or child abductor. Maybe he would go to the mixer. Occasionally, the girls in the office had invited him along on their nights out, probably because they felt sorry for him or thought he was gay. He resolved to go the next time he was asked. Maybe he should tell them he *was* gay. Maybe that would go a little toward explaining some obvious gaps he'd have when talking about his personal life.

There were some questions for the aliens and he asked them, waiting for them to emit a response. While he was eager to get started, he didn't want to be too hasty. He had to know what he was doing. He had to know what he could expect to get out of this.

The questions were asked and the answers were given in the coming weeks.

How often would he be expected to do this?

It was hard to say. It would depend on need and transportation. Alexander's earth was not always open to these beings. He would be given advance notice and the beings would appropriately coordinate their arrival.

Would the children have to be alive?

That was not really an issue. As long as there wasn't significant deterioration of the tissue, the beings would be able to use them.

Why did they want children?

Research.

Male or female?

It didn't matter. Preferably both so they could study reproduction and the differences in the sexes.

Would Alexander ever see them again?

Possibly. If he did what the beings asked, and did a good

job, there may be a special place reserved for him.

Would there be any bodies? Any evidence to cover up?

They would take care of that.

What if he got caught?

That was outside their capabilities of control. He should take every precaution.

On June 1st of that year, Alexander abducted a boy named Max Hamlisch from a small rural town just north of Columbus. The boy was walking his dog along a road just before sundown. Alexander bashed the dog's head in with a tire iron, snapped the boy's neck, and tossed him in the trunk of his car. In the woods behind the house in Twin Springs, he stripped the boy naked, violated his corpse, put the boy's clothes back on, and left the body there. Alexander didn't hear anything about it.

The next month he took a boy from a Pittsburgh suburb.

Over the next six years, there would be 43 more children. If he should ever want to abuse their bodies for too long, there was always the voice of the beings reminding him what a valuable asset he was to them. There was also the fear of recrimination and punishment. Although the more he got away with it, the more invincible Alexander felt. Most of them were boys. A few of them were girls. They were all between the ages of ten and twelve.

With the exception of one boy getting away, everything had gone off without a hitch until that night, exactly seven years later, when he left a dead boy in the woods, swerved to avoid a deer standing in the middle of the road, and lost control of his car.

He emerged from the car without really thinking. He could walk fine. He gave himself a pat down and didn't seem to be bleeding from anywhere. He felt more like he was in a daze, almost like he was outside of himself. He staggered to the house he remembered from his childhood. It was the place he'd been in least of all, and yet it was the one most seared into his memory. There had been the house where he'd lived with his mother and father. Then his father had run off and he and his mother had moved to this house in Twin Springs where they lived for no more than a year. Then, probably because of the troubles his mother was having with him, they'd gone to live with his grandparents in Glowers Hook.

Alexander approached the door to the house and everything went kind of blank for a while.

He was pretty sure he needed help.

He hoped these people could help him.

Shortly after entering the house there was a bright flash of light that seemed to simultaneously suck everything out of the air while also infusing it with some form of wild energy. That would be the aliens, he thought, coming to claim their human child.

3.

The man continued to sit on the couch, his hands resting on his knees, staring straight ahead at the dead television. His lips were moving but nothing was coming out of his mouth. Thinking he was trying to talk, Slade asked, "Huh?" the first couple of times. The Brothers Brian had quieted down on the patio.

Slade crouched by the wall outlet. Sometimes when the battery ran out completely, it took the phone a couple of minutes to come to life again even when connected to the wall. Since the lights to the house were still on (maybe there had been a brief flicker) he didn't see any reason why this shouldn't work. Unless everything was fried. That would suck hugely. He wondered if he could get renter's insurance to cover something like that. If it worked, that would be great. That meant he could get his camera running and at least record a few minutes of this weird guy. He thought it could be the beginning of one of those documentaries that said as much about the director as it did the subject. Start with this weird, pale, hairless guy sitting on his couch mumbling and work backward from there. Why was he here? Where had he been going? Why was he hairless? The reasons were probably mundane, but it was this beauty in mundaneness or in the quiet captured moments of great extraordinariness that seemed to resonate with indie audiences.

Slade glanced down at his phone. Still no sign of life.

He had not set out to make fuck videos. He wanted to make a living in the arts and this seemed to be the easiest way. He had grown up in the rural town of Glowers Hook, Ohio, and later enrolled in the film program at Wright State. He'd done well and his senior project was much lauded. His professor encouraged him to enroll it in some film festivals. On top of his already sizeable student loans he knew he was going to have to pay back some day, he had taken a bank loan to pay the entrance fees to all the festivals he was to enter it in. He did this for about a year, living with his parents and working on a feature length script. The film was accepted into most of the festivals it was entered in. It was rejected from South by Southwest and Sundance, the two he was *real-*

ly hoping it would be accepted into. Being accepted into either of those would have probably gained him more exposure than winning a grand prize at all the other ones combined. It did take the grand prize at a small festival in Tukwila, Washington, and a "silver" prize at a festival in East Lansing, Michigan. He hadn't attended either of them and was surprised at the film's success. Both of them awarded modest prize money that amounted to only about three times the entrance fee. He was still in touch with his university professor and asked him for advice. Well, his professor said, if he was really serious about filmmaking, he'd need to move out to LA. So Slade took what was left of the loan and his prize money and moved to LA, where he shared an apartment with three other forgettable film school graduates. He shopped his script around to agents and tried to get a distribution deal for his student film. He was met with rejection for the following year. Finally he said fuck it and uploaded his film to YouTube while continuing to shop his wares. It sat there for a year where he obsessively checked its view count. It never got above 400. One night, he drunkenly made a POV film of himself fucking his girlfriend at the time and uploaded it to a porn site. By the end of the week it had over 400,000 views on that site alone. He was pretty sure it had spread itself around to other sites too. His face wasn't in it. His girlfriend wasn't as upset as he thought she would be. She left him and accepted the many, many offers that came her way. He shifted focus. Hired people to design and manage a website. Ultimately he left LA because he realized he could do the same thing back home for a fraction of the price. The women in LA wanted too much money and a lot of them thought it was a stepping stone to some fabulous career. He couldn't afford to pay them and he couldn't afford to keep paying his lawyers to fend off their lawyers. Back in Ohio, there was still enough shame attached to it that he hadn't been sued once in the three years he'd been doing this. And girls worked for about a fourth the price plus drugs. Drugs had been somewhat of a given in LA too. But even their drugs were more expensive. In Twin Springs, he could get a girl high on pot, film an hour long video where he fucked the girl in the ass and finished in her mouth, send her away with a couple hundred bucks and they felt like they'd won the lottery and were now definitely the hippest one amongst all their friends and might even get famous to boot. That video, through advertiser revenue, would earn him around 20,000 dollars, of which he would retain around sixty percent. Not bad. You just had to watch out for their boyfriends. That never happened in LA. The guys just didn't care and, if they wanted to, the girls probably wouldn't let them.

Of course, he wouldn't have to worry about any of that if all of his fucking equipment was fried.

His phone still had not blinked to life and the man on the couch was now not just moving his lips but whispering.

Slade couldn't make out any of the words.

It almost sounded like he was chanting but there was a nearly electronic sound coming from his mouth.

Still nothing from his phone.

Slade was not an overly superstitious person, but he thought maybe if he just walked away from it, it would happen. Plus he needed to get away from that sound.

He walked to the carport door and glanced out.

Sierra's car was still out there.

Of course it was. The battery was probably dead.

He considered going out to check on her and then thought, *Fuck it.*

He stood in the doorway and watched the man on the couch. He considered telling him to keep it down, the chanting had grown so loud. What had gone from being an inconvenience to a major pain in the ass was now quickly escalating into a situation that was starting to creep him out.

Obviously there was something off about the guy. Something that went beyond shock. Besides that, though . . . there was something *familiar* about this guy. At first he'd thought it was perhaps the most notable thing – the complete absence of hair. But Slade knew he'd never met anyone with that . . . was it a condition or a preference? He didn't know. Then he thought maybe it was the blank expression in the eyes. And it *was* a familiar expression, but had nothing to do with the bearer. He'd filmed enough scenes with girls who'd had one, maybe two partners in her life before suddenly getting her ass fucked by the biggest cock she would ever see in person while simultaneously having another huge cock shoved down her throat. Yeah, some of them looked a little dazed and blank afterward. Especially when this went on past the point of pain or pleasure and into numb grinding muscle movement.

He moved closer to the man. Maybe if he placed a gentle hand on him and calmly asked him to quiet down, the guy would stop.

Slade glanced at his phone on the floor as he crossed the room. Still nothing.

He would have to ask one of the Brians to go to the police station or sit here with the guy while he did. He was feeling so freaked out right now he almost wished they *would* refuse to go.

He crouched down in front of the stranger and put his hand on his knee.

"Sir?"

Those sounds continued to come from his mouth. Slade had almost grown used to them. It was almost like they *didn't* actually come from his mouth but were made somewhere in his head and poured from his nostrils.

From this lower angle, Slade noticed his nostrils for the first time. One was round. One was tear-shaped.

Just as it all came back to him, he heard White Brian say, "What the fuck!"

Slade turned to look out the window to the backyard and saw them.

4.

That morning, it was like an alarm had gone off in William Tanner's head. William was twelve. He sometimes had weird thoughts but never with as much clarity as he had this one. It was like, for whatever question he had for the voice, the answer immediately waited for him.

What about Mom?

She will understand.

How will I find this place?

You'll just know.

How long will it take?

You will make it in time, if you leave now.

He pushed his chair back from the table and said to his mother, standing at the sink washing the waffle iron, "I have to go."

She turned, looking vaguely startled. "Where do you have to go? Nothing's open."

"I have to go," he repeated. Only this time it sounded like other sounds came out as well. It sounded a lot like the sounds that sometimes went with his weird thoughts.

His mother's expression changed. From that wide-eyed startled look to something like resigned horror.

He got his bike out of the garage, hopped on, and rode it to Twin Springs, Ohio.

Chris Hizer didn't bother telling his mom he was leaving. This was a couple days before William left. Chris lived in Colorado and the only mode of transportation he had was a skateboard. It was going to take a while.

When darkness came to the Hizer household, it was his stepfather who finally said he was getting worried.

"I'm sure he'll be okay," his mother said.

His stepdad protested before finally acquiescing. He never really liked Chris anyway. He was creepy. One of the creepiest eleven-year-olds he'd ever met.

Penny Mugwump didn't need to tell her mother she was leaving. She no longer had one. Penny was going to tell her. She went into her mother's bedroom to tell her but she couldn't get her to wake up. Penny thought about calling 911 but the voice in her head told her she didn't really have time to do that, plus she'd have to answer a lot of questions. Not that Penny had anything to do with her mother's death. Nor did she know what heroin was. Her mother called it her medicine and said she needed it to relax. Most of the time her mother's medicine used to involved taking a pill or smoking out of a little pipe. This seemed to involve a lot more stuff.

Not that it really mattered now anyway.

Penny had a pretty strong feeling she wouldn't be coming back to her tiny house in Evanston, Illinois, anyway. She hopped on her tricycle – sadly, the only thing she had – and headed to Twin Springs, Ohio, a pretty good jaunt for a twelve-year-old girl with asthma.

5.

Slade had been eleven the last time he'd seen the man on the couch. He hadn't called himself Slade then. He was just Tyler Grimm, a small town kid with no hopes or ambitions. One ambition he knew he *didn't* have was to be kidnapped and raped by a pervert.

He'd been at the park playing baseball with his friends. This was in Glowers Hook, so the park was pretty much surrounded by woods. It would have been an ideal place for drug deals to go down, along with all kinds of other unsavory acts. But that was practically every park in this area and somehow the reputation had escaped this one. Pickle Park was what they called the one by the river where every alleged homosexual in the tri-state region met to do whatever faggots did. It would take Tyler a long time to stop thinking about them that way but that was pretty much the accepted terminology for that area of Ohio at that time.

They'd finished packing up their equipment and his friends had left him behind. Ben was already late and Layne always gave Tyler a hard time for being so slow. He would shout "Lollygagger!" and dart out of the house, often while Tyler was still tying his shoes.

He didn't think they would have left him if they'd seen the gray Honda parked in the small parking lot.

"Hey kid!" a man called as he got out of the car.

Tyler hoisted his aluminum bat onto his shoulder, his glove looped over the knob at the end of the handle, and began walking toward the entrance of the park. He thought it was best if he pretended not to hear him.

"Kid, wait up!" the man called.

Tyler kept walking. But . . . there was something in his head telling him not to. It told him he should stop. It told him he should stop and do whatever this man wanted him to do.

But he knew this voice wasn't right.

What would Natalie think if something happened to him? She was his thirteen-year-old neighbor but she had finally let him do what he'd been begging to do for the past three months. It was every bit as good as he thought it would be, although he wasn't sure if she thought so or not. It hadn't taken very long and she had cried afterward. Nevertheless, she had a kind of power over him now.

Tyler walked faster.

He could hear the guy behind him.

"Hey kid, wait up! I just want you to help me figure out where I'm at!"

The guy was now practically right behind him.

Maybe he wasn't a creep, Tyler thought, but wondered why he would try to get directions from a kid on a playground rather than in town or at a gas station.

Tyler stopped and turned around. Maybe the guy was legit. If he wanted to grab him, he was close enough to do so anyway. He would answer the guy's question but if he reached for him he was going to clobber him with the bat, which he now gripped very tightly.

The man stopped short.

"Thanks, little guy," he said. Tyler wasn't really that little.

Now, facing the man, he thought the guy looked weird. He had these different shaped nostrils but that wasn't the least of it. The man wore what had to be a wig under a hat that had a graphic of a police badge and the letters F.O.P. on it. And his eyebrows were clearly drawn on. And not well. It looked like whatever he'd used was already running down the man's face with his sweat.

So it's easy to wash off, Tyler thought just as the man reached out. He didn't know where that thought had come from.

Tyler didn't take the time to pull the bat back and administer a proper swing. He just rammed it forward into the guy's crotch and took off running in the opposite direction, yelling "Help!" the entire time.

It was a pretty rural area and when Tyler hit the road he was the only one on it. He heard the car crunch on the gravel of the park's lot, which meant the man was pulling out, and Tyler threw himself into the woods on his right. Under camouflage, he watched the road. He saw the front of the car pull out of the parking lot and head in the opposite direction.

Tyler sat down in the dirt, his heart hammering. He still felt uneasy but he also felt a sense of relief.

When he got home he told his mom about the encounter. She called the police and an officer came out to ask him questions and file a report. He felt nearly famous for a week or two. He also felt like the luckiest boy in the world.

Even though his mother had never mentioned his biological father, Tyler asked her, "Do you think that could have been my real dad, come back for me?"

She had rubbed his head and said she didn't think he'd ever see that guy again. He wasn't sure if she meant the creep or his dad who, he guessed, was also a creep. They probably weren't the same person. The truth, which she would never tell him but he somehow knew just by glancing into her eyes, was that she had no idea how she'd gotten pregnant. Someone would have had to have broken into her house, drugged her and raped her, all without her knowledge. She wasn't a slut. She didn't go to parties. She wasn't a virgin but it had been months since she'd had sex. She maybe remembered having morning sickness but didn't go to the doctor until her belly became distended and hard. She was afraid she had a tumor or some kind of intestinal disorder. The doctor informed her that she was probably seven months pregnant.

She told Tyler he would never see that guy again.

Now Tyler, who called himself Slade, thought his mother was wrong.

6.

"I'm not helping you," Slade said to the man.

The man's volume had increased. His eyes stared straight forward and looked filled with fear.

Slade still did not think of this man as his father. He thought of the creep who'd tried to do something to him when he was just a kid.

The light from outside was flashing, closer, making it hard to think. Shapes moved amidst the light. Maybe Sierra *had* gone to the police.

But why would they be coming through the woods?

Slade stood slowly, wanting away from the man. Now he *had* to go to the police. Who knew how many times the man in front of him had tried to do what he did to him. How many times had he been successful?

He went toward the patio door. He needed to tell the Brothers Brian to keep an eye out on this guy and to not let him leave under any circumstances.

He also needed to find out what that light was.

It was so intense it felt like it was burning a hole somewhere in his brain.

He opened the back door.

The Brothers Brian were in the chairs on the patio only . . . they had changed. Slade smelled burning. Their bodies were molten lumps, blood and unidentifiable ooze dripping from the straps of the chairs.

But Slade was having trouble making out anything.

That light. Flashing. And each flash seemed to be accompanied with some kind of heaviness that made him feel like collapsing.

But he had a sense of purpose.

He could not see into the light but, when he closed his eyes, he saw a lingering afterimage of shapes.

What the fuck was going on?

The light was so bright it illuminated the inside of the house so Slade was able to look in and see the strange man. He now stood in the middle of the living room, his arms raised to the ceiling and, even from outside, Slade could hear that alien chanting coming from him.

Slade didn't want to go back inside.

Fuck his phone. Fuck his camera. He didn't even care about going to the police at this point. He ran around the west side of the house and stopped under the cover of the carport.

There were kids.

A lot of them.

Coming down the road in front of his house. There were at least 25 to 30 of them. They all looked young. Some of them were on bikes. Some of them were on skateboards. One had ridden a moped. Another a go-kart. One girl was on a tricycle that seemed way too small for her. Some of them were on foot. If they had one, they discarded their particular mode of transportation at the guardrail that ended Spring Street. They walked purposefully toward the house. Their eyes all shone with the blinding light that Slade now thought came from the sky. He staggered out of the carport and into the side yard. He didn't know if he was looking for an umbrella from all that glaring light or if he just wanted to be away from the house. What if whatever had happened to the Brothers Brian happened to him?

He heard sounds coming from the backyard, from the woods. It was the last earthly sound he heard.

More kids were coming from the woods. These had been the shapes he had seen. Now, as they moved closer to him, he could see their bodies glowing with the same light coming from the other kids' eyes.

Now he heard a sound like a low flying military carrier only a thousand times more intense.

The light was so bright everything looked flattened and bleached.

The children were joining hands around the house.

The house's windows shattered. Not hearing it, only seeing it, made Slade feel oddly disconnected.

Two children came toward him. One had the glowing eyes. The other had the glowing body. They held out their hands. Slade felt terrified but also strangely elated.

He let the children help him up. Their touch sent a strange current of calm through him. It was something he wasn't sure he'd ever felt before.

He joined the circle around the house.

The house was being flattened. It reminded Slade of a tornado but the pressure seemed super concentrated. Flattened and shredded, the house spiraled in the middle of their circle before being sucked up into the sky like some kind of demolished house soup.

The odd man stood in the middle of the circle, still shouting, his hands raised.

Slade felt like they were somehow helping this man and wanted to be away from the circle until –

7.

They were finally coming for him, Alexander thought.

The house was lifted away from him and he saw it disappear into the bright light. He saw all of his accomplishments, both past and future, surrounding him. All of his children, harvested from him that one night.

He felt those things reach into his head. He'd always remained open to them.

He knew he had been a sick man.

Sometimes he'd tried to convince himself they were the reason for this sickness.

What people saw as his sickness was really his earthly reward for doing their deeds. He wanted to shout at them he had taken what he deserved.

Before everything went black, he tried to recall what it had been like the last time. He'd never felt anything like it since although he'd certainly tried. He closed his eyes and wished to go back.

8.

– the man's clothes were ripped from his body. His flesh was ripped away from the bone just as easily until he was only a skeleton and the skeleton became so much dust, invisible in all that bright light.

Slade couldn't think about anything over that deafening vacuum roar. It felt like the ground was lifting beneath his feet. Maybe he was going somewhere. He didn't want to go anywhere. He wanted to stay here. He wanted to suck everything he possibly could from life. But he couldn't move.

The circle rose toward that white light.

Suddenly everything was calm and peaceful.

Slade wondered if he would ever get used to it. He wondered if he could go back. There were colors and feelings but it all seemed too subtle and ethereal. He thought about flesh sliding against flesh. The sharp sting of pain. The explosions of pleasure. The lingering feeling in the soul of what it means to be in pain and what it means to hurt someone else.

That was what he wanted his life to be. A human life. In the midst of all that black sorrow there were pink explosions of joy and happiness. That was what he lived for.

He didn't know what this was.

He felt the alien sensation of something entering his head. It was like that voice he'd heard in the park that day. Uninvited. Unwanted. It felt . . . unedited was the only way he could think to describe it.

He had been the missing link in the circle. What would have happened to him if he'd stayed outside of it? Would he have died? Was *this* death?

He tried to quit thinking.

He tried to give himself to it.

But he just kept wondering if his world would ever come back to him.

Other Grindhouse Press Titles

#666__*Satanic Summer* by Andersen Prunty

#021__*Other People's Shit* by C.V. Hunt

#020__*The Party Lords* by Justin Grimbol

#019__*Sociopaths In Love* by Andersen Prunty

#018__*The Last Porno Theater* by Nick Cato

#017__*Zombieville* by C.V. Hunt

#016__*Samurai Vs. Robo-Dick* by Steve Lowe

#015__*The Warm Glow of Happy Homes* by Andersen Prunty

#014__*How To Kill Yourself* by C.V. Hunt

#013__*Bury the Children in the Yard: Horror Stories* by Andersen Prunty

#012 __*Return to Devil Town (Vampires in Devil Town Book Three)* by Wayne Hixon

#011__*Pray You Die Alone: Horror Stories* by Andersen Prunty

#010__*King of the Perverts* by Steve Lowe

#009__*Sunruined: Horror Stories* by Andersen Prunty

#008__*Bright Black Moon: Vampires in Devil Town Book Two* by Wayne Hixon

#007__*Hi I'm a Social Disease: Horror Stories* by Andersen Prunty

#006__*A Life On Fire* by Chris Bowsman

#005__*The Sorrow King* by Andersen Prunty

#004__*The Brothers Crunk* by William Pauley III

#003__*The Horribles* by Nathaniel Lambert

#002__*Vampires in Devil Town* by Wayne Hixon

#001__*House of Fallen Trees* by Gina Ranalli

#000__*Morning is Dead* by Andersen Prunty